THE HOUNDS OF SPRING

THE HOUNDS
OF SPRING

LUCY ANDREWS CUMMIN

Leapfolio

A joint-venture partner of Tupelo Press
North Adams, Massachusetts

Library of Congress Cataloging-in-Publication Data

Names: Cummin, Lucy Andrews, author.
Title: The hounds of spring / Lucy Andrews Cummin.
Description: North Adams, Massachusetts : Leapfolio,
a joint-venture partner of Tupelo Press, [2017]
Identifiers: LCCN 2017042572 | ISBN 9781946507020 (alk. paper)
Subjects: LCSH: Dog walking—Fiction.
Classification: LCC PS3603.U654 H68 2017 | DDC 813/.6—dc23
LC record available at https://lccn.loc.gov/2017042572

ISBN: 978-1-946507-02-0

Cover and text designed by Margery Cantor.
Text is set in Arno Pro with Castellar titling.
Cover art: "Lucy with Three Dogs," by Carolyn Mecklosky.
Copyright © 2017, licensed by Leapfolio. Used with permission.

First edition: March 2018.

Leapfolio, a joint-venture partner of Tupelo Press
P.O. Box 1767, North Adams, Massachusetts 01247
(413) 664–9611 / info@leapfolio.net / www.leapfolio.net

for Knox,
our daughter, Elizabeth,
and
the sublime
Periwinkle

CONTENTS

When the hounds of spring are on winter's traces,
    The mother of months in meadow or plain
Fills the shadows and windy places
    With lisp of leaves and ripple of rain;
And the brown bright nightingale amorous
Is half assuaged for Itylus,
For the Thracian ships and the foreign faces,
    The tongueless vigil, and all the pain.

Come with bows bent and with emptying of quivers,
    Maiden most perfect, lady of light,
With a noise of winds and many rivers,
    With a clamour of waters, and with might;
Bind on thy sandals, O thou most fleet,
Over the splendour and speed of thy feet;
For the faint east quickens, the wan west shivers,
    Round the feet of the day and the feet of the night.

from a chorus in "Atalanta in Calydon"
by Charles Algernon Swinburne

THE HOUNDS OF SPRING

MORNING

THE FIRST ORDER OF BUSINESS was to let Spock out into the very small backyard. This morning while he nosed about, Poppy watched from the very small wooden deck Clive had built last summer, admiring the pansies and primroses he had planted in terra cotta pots over the weekend. She was thinking about how different they were. Clive liked to be busy. He liked to go from one thing to the next. He was the same at home as at work. He was happy.

She was happy with Clive, but she was not happy with herself.

Her first choice of career had failed and she had fallen into wandering the city and woods, dogs as her companions, with time to note how a tree wrote its history in its bark or a family revealed their state in the condition and decoration of their front door. What was unnerving was that this life suited her quite well and she was even being paid, but it was a stopgap. After almost two years it was getting to be a very long stopgap.

Spock returned, tail wagging, tongue lolling, lifting his upper lip slightly so only the gums showed; his imitation of a human smile. They went in.

Her breakfast today was yogurt with nuts and blueberries. Early morning was her best time and breakfast her favorite meal. No one asked, "Shall we have green beans or peas? Pasta or potatoes? Beef or chicken?" No one remarked, "Haven't we had brown rice and chicken the past five nights?" Best of all, she was alone, so there was no scattering of dreams or diminishment of the day's potential.

Poppy liked breakfast so much that she was apt to slip like a leaf diverted into a quiet shallows, spinning lazily, until the prickling sense of time passing made her consult a clock.

"Oh no! I'm late!" She would leap up, startling Spock, hurriedly washing her bowl and spoon, running around in search of keys, pouring coffee into her commuter mug, stuffing a water bottle, along with a carrot, cheese, and crackers into a bag for a sort of lunch, a book, and her appointment book where she wrote down her visits and hours. All too frequently she had to come back for something. On a very bad day she came back more than once.

She didn't know, but Clive would always listen to see how many times the door slammed, an accurate indicator of her state of being.

Poppy's regular clients were Penelope, Fauna, Horatio, Bliss, and Chutney, often with, as was the plan today, a final stop around noon to check in on Mrs. Twigg, who was presently without a dog, which was a worry. Tucked into today's agenda at two thirty would be Clive's follow-up appointment with the heart specialist.

In the front hall, Poppy paused to put on her jacket and a scarf of thin chiffon fabric patterned with irises. Opening the front door she stepped out into spring, the one season of glory Philadelphia offers. Two months of near perfection: April, crisp and sweet, and May, almost an overdose of blooms and blossoms, scents, zephyrs, and delights.

Today was classic April. Brisk and bright but not at all wintery. The crocuses she and Clive had planted around their little tree, a London plane, were quite spent and the daffodils were pushing up green shoots with fat tips of a lighter green.

Poppy stood on the marble stoop and surveyed the street. People in this neighborhood were sloppy with their trash, noisy on weekend nights (and sporadically on others), found it sporting to smash their empties wherever, and stole anything not firmly lashed down. Behind lace curtains old ladies knew exactly who had done what to whom and when. Two streets south a wide avenue was rapidly gentrifying; the pressure could already be felt. Poppy and Clive knew they were the vanguard. Outsiders. On the corner a seedy pub had finally closed, and one with pretensions for this neighborhood—decent hamburgers, soups, and salads, as well as foreign beers and wine by the glass—had appeared. Better yet, the retiled and plumbed bathrooms didn't smell of anything but air freshener. At the other end of the block, a contractor was rehabbing a large three-story house into condos with parking round back, where only a year ago there had still been a row of disintegrating cars. Clive was maddened by the fact that, however shoddy the work, the condos would sell for the parking.

All was quiet. The windows of Poppy's 1966 Vista Cruiser Oldsmobile were intact, as they should be, since she didn't ever lock the car. Opening the door behind the driver's seat she put her black canvas bag on the litter-strewn floor, then opened the driver's door to perch her coffee mug on the dash.

Before heading out on her rounds Poppy always walked Spock around the block to prove that he was *the most special dog of all.* Spock, trotting a couple of yards in front of her, was as usual leashless; he had come into Poppy's life fully trained. On a one-word command or a hand gesture he would sit; he did his business on the street by the curb and came punctiliously when called. She believed he extrapolated when confronted with a new situation, flawlessly choosing the behavior he deemed appropriate (anything from sitting, growling, or moving protectively closer to her). For the most part he ignored all other dogs and barked so rarely that when he did she paid attention. People were impressed, but Poppy couldn't take the credit.

Being Poppy's first committed adult relationship, Spock deserves to have his story told.

Before Clive, Poppy was living in a house with several other between-college-and-the-next-thing friends from high school near but not in University City. She was a graduate student in literature at a university north of New York, which was in a city she disliked, so she commuted by train once a week for two days and one night of classes and meetings.

The trouble had escalated when the time came to settle on a dissertation topic. She proposed to investigate what makes James Boswell feel so contemporary, including his self-absorption, his obsessiveness, his celebrity-seeking strategems. Her advisor rejected her chosen topic as "fanciful." Her advisor was The Expert, and most of the journals of Boswell were in the possession of his university because decades ago an alumnus had found a stash of them hidden in an old chest in the attic of a house he was living in. After that find, he begged descendants of Boswell to let him explore their attics, and he had arranged for his alma mater to purchase the papers. This professor, then a graduate student and now very elderly, had been painstakingly deciphering, editing, notating, and publishing the journals ever since. Credit where due, this man did brilliant and meticulous work.

He suggested she explore Boswell's relations with the women in his life, a subject that did not much interest him or her. When she said no, he said, "I thought you women were all fighting for this sort of thing."

"Actually no," Poppy said, trying to stay calm, "The opposite. Would you recommend this subject to a male student?"

The professor stared at his blotter and did not answer her. Then he said, "I was trying to find a suitable topic for you. If this is not acceptable then I suggest you consider applying your . . . imagination to writing fiction. Your own idea is dependent on speculation as opposed to scholarship. The scholarly life is not for everyone. It requires objectivity, attention to detail, and devotion to facts, all of which you appear to lack."

No one so far, in her whole life, had spoken to Poppy with such blunt condescension and she was struck speechless. Was this what is meant by putting a woman in her place? Was he implying that women are too subjective to make good scholars or just her? He didn't *have* any other female students so how could she know what he meant? There was a committee, but this professor had them all well in hand. If he said no, they would also. There was no appeal.

The professor's hands were clasped on his desk and he was barely hiding a little smile. He had known how she would react and he would be glad to be rid of her.

The worst of it was, as she rose and with all the dignity she could muster left the room, she knew he was probably right. She loved the literature, but it wasn't enough. If he was what she had to aspire to becoming, this was not the career for her.

She didn't get in a last word, but she had had the satisfaction of slamming his office door hard enough to shatter the opaque glass window.

For most of the following year, when not at her restaurant job, Poppy lay on the sofa in the living room of the shared house, rereading all the books that had inspired her to think of becoming a scholar of eighteenth-century literature: Fielding (and his sister Sarah), Smollett, Richardson, Boswell, Johnson, Swift, Goldsmith, Defoe, de Quincey. Something about the way these writers thought and wrote continued to thrill and excite her. While Victorians from Eliot to James often felt remote, the irreverent sensibilities of these writers felt immediate and comprehensible, modern, contemporary, and Boswell most of all. She had wanted so much to explore why.

She also read everything else she came across, from contemporary literature to mysteries and fantasy.

Friends and family either consoled or chided, reminding her "these things happen"—you trained as a park ranger and then found yourself not in the wilderness counting bears or preventing forest fires but herding tourists in Independence Hall Park.

The reality was she had disliked graduate school, which she had found to be weirdly like sixth grade. Her fellow students had been accomplished and subtle masters of the tangential put-down, the unexpected backstabbing, the gossipy and damning innuendo. You couldn't mention that you knew episodes of *Star Trek* by heart or that you had never even *heard* of *Dallas*. If you weren't familiar with every one of Luis Bunuel's films, you were, put simply, a loser. Hitchcock was acceptable in discussions only if you approached his work mockingly. To admit you loved your area of study was suicidal.

That was over, so the problem was what to do?

In the meantime she had a decent gig as a wait*person* at a hip restaurant near the University of Pennsylvania.

In those days, B.C. (Before Clive), Poppy had no transportation and walked home alone, probably a stupid thing to do, but there was no workable bus, none of her colleagues lived in her direction and she didn't like to ask for a ride unless it was raining hard or snowing. Most of the twenty-minute hike went through what might reasonably be called an okay neighborhood of large Victorian-era duplexes shaded by sycamores and oaks, favored by full professors (who owned) and married graduate students and adjuncts with families (who rented). This more prosperous area was bordered on two sides, north and west, by two indisputably lousy neighborhoods. To the south were the two huge universities, Drexel and Penn; eastward lay the railroad, expressway, and river. The house she and her friends rented was on the western cusp of the acceptable neighborhoods.

Then one balmy late summer night when she was about halfway home, a medium-size dark-coated dog of indeterminate breed and gender trotted out of a side yard and attached itself to Poppy's left leg, heeling perfectly. She stopped and the dog stopped and sat down. "You need to go home," she said. By lamplight she saw the dog was brown and black with fur not long or short. The dog raised its head slightly and she could see the gleam of a honey-brown eye in the streetlight. Its ears were upright, with floppy, feathered tips. She saw a gleam of tooth, only it was not a baring of fangs, but the canine imitation of a friendly human grin. "I'm serious!" Poppy said, but at the same time, as she'd been taught, she had held out her hand for the dog to sniff, which it licked with the grace of a regency gentleman kissing a gloved hand. She was convinced then that the dog was male. She felt around his neck for a collar, finding it bare, but with the roughness of scar tissue, where the collar should have been.

"All right," Poppy said. "Suit yourself. I could use a bodyguard." The dog walked her home, his slightly plumed tail waving slowly, a sign, she knew, of contentment. When he lifted a leg to casually sprinkle a hydrant what she had already decided was confirmed. When she got home the dog came right up onto the porch with her and stood expectantly at the door. "I can't let you in," Poppy said. "You're not my dog. You should go home."

In the end, she left him on the porch with a bowl of water. Before going up to bed she peeked out the bay window of the living room and saw that the dog had made himself at home on the ratty cushioned seat of the wicker sofa left outside all year round. In the morning, to her relief (tinged with a disappointment she barely admitted to herself), he was gone.

For a few nights there was no sign of him, but then he reappeared. From then on this handsome, self-possessed dog, always collarless, always in the same general vicinity, appeared and accompanied Poppy home every few days. She broke down and bought a box of dog biscuits to give him along with the water.

Soon, before going up to bed, Poppy began sitting with the dog on the porch sofa, his head resting on her lap, her mind fully at rest. The fact was she liked dogs, *really* liked dogs. And dogs liked her. At home, her mother, who liked to promote legends about her children's various talents and proclivities, always said that when they brought Poppy home from the hospital, the family dog, a lab named Bianca, had abandoned her dog basket in the master bedroom and moved under her crib.

Poppy never let the dog in, and in the morning he was always gone. She was careful not to let herself think of a name for him. As much as he apparently wished he was and as she was beginning to wish for as well, he was not her dog.

One miserable January night Poppy couldn't bear to leave the dog on the porch and took him up to her room. She checked him over carefully for fleas but did not find any, and other than a small notch in one ear and that rawness around his neck, he seemed decently cared for. He went to sleep on the small rug by her bed, but in the morning he was lying beside her, his head raised and his eyes on her, as if he had been watching her sleep. The message couldn't have been clearer. *I have chosen you.* That day she bought some dog food. After that when he came home with her she let him in and fed him and rose very early to let him out.

In early March, winter relented and Poppy was letting the dog out in the dark of early morning when she heard the squeak of a vehicle door opening across the street. A very large balding man jumped out of an air-conditioning repair van with the slogan, *Let Us Help You Keep Your Cool.* She turned to go inside.

The man ran toward her shouting, "Hey!" She stopped, turning back.

Having seen the man, the dog hesitated, revealing an uncertainty Poppy had never before seen him show; he looked ready to either bolt down the street or run back to Poppy with his tail between his legs. Afraid.

The man yelled, "Rocky! Sit!" The dog sat. Poppy understood that the dog would have let himself be run over rather than disobey this man. All sensation left her arms and legs and she couldn't breathe.

Then the man started yelling at her.

"Who the *fuck* do you think you are? Stealing my dog? Shoulda known it would be some goddamned cunt." He went on like this. Poppy stood paralyzed.

The man picked up the dog as if he was stuffed with styrofoam peanuts.

The dog looked at Poppy radiating shame and misery.

Holding the dog in his arms, the man stood at the foot of the stairs. "So what the fuck, bitch?"

Fury replaced her fear. In the plays she used to put on with her siblings, she was always the governess or the headmistress; she had found that a version of this voice was effective at the restaurant at deflating rude customers.

Recklessly, Poppy stepped right to the edge of the porch and looked down at him and said in her steeliest voice, "Your dog follows me home. He has no tags and no I.D. Would you have preferred I call the pound?"

Clive called this her "Back atchoo, asshole" voice.

"Just leave my dog the fuck alone," the man said, blinking rapidly.

"And how would I do that?" She relented slightly, as if she genuinely wanted to know.

Still standing there the man shifted from one foot to the other and said, now confiding and plaintive, "Shoulda named him Houdini. I bought, like, fifty collars. He can get out of anything."

"Wow," Poppy said.

Instantly the man became almost jolly! "I guess I know where to find him next time, hunh?"

"Yes," she said. "If you like, you can leave your phone number."

But he turned away, waving a dismissive hand, saying, "Nah, let Rocky out like you were doing already," and still carrying the dog, he got in his van and left.

After the incident with his owner, the dog appeared almost every night, as if the man had given up on trying to keep him penned or chained. He was still "the dog," Poppy wouldn't call him Rocky and she didn't like the idea of Houdini. The man did not come back.

Then one Saturday afternoon in June, as she was about to leave for work, the man was there, sitting on her stoop, and he had the dog beside him. The dog was wearing a new collar and leash, and there was half a bag of dog food and a beat-up metal bowl.

"I'm moving to Florida," the man said. "I'm in a hurry and I can't take him. I'll sell him to you."

The man asked for an absurd amount of money, but Poppy didn't argue. She went to her room, got what he asked for from her hidden stash and handed him the cash.

He was still "the dog" in early July when Clive came into her life. She was in a park near the Philadelphia Art Museum throwing a ball for the dog, and instead of bringing it back to her he took the ball to Clive, who was sitting on a bench, drawing, dropping it on the paper propped in his lap. The fourth or fifth time Clive had to pick up the thoroughly slobbered item, he wiped his hands and put his drawing pad and pencils away, stood up, and said, "Let's play keep-away from *him*."

"He is like Mr. Spock," Clive said as they lay in bed a week or two later contemplating him. "He has pointy ears and he is logical and probably telepathic. I was looking at you thinking, from the way you were playing with him, you had to be a nice person. I think he knew that; he's protective of you, concerned about you, but he knows he's a dog. He's not jealous of me like a confused dog might be."

"He chose me. Now he has chosen you," Poppy said. "Spock is a good name for him."

After becoming Poppy's dog, Spock never ran away again. Sadly, since she couldn't take him to work, she had to walk home alone once more. Except not really, because before long Clive started picking her up. If they were going to his place on the other side of University City they would stop at hers to get Spock, who would somehow always know they were coming to get him, and would be waiting at the door.

The saga of Spock gave Poppy's mother the idea to give her daughter's phone number to an elderly friend, Irene Childress, who had mentioned she needed help with her dog. Irene had recommended her to someone else, and so on. Now Poppy had five regular dog-walking clients and the occasional weekender. She had quit the restaurant when she and Clive (mostly Clive) bought a house across the river, closer to Center City. The dog-walking gig wasn't quite a livelihood but in the circumstances was close enough for the time being. She was, after all, supposed to be figuring out what she was *really* going to do with her life.

As Poppy turned the corner she became aware that her mind was drifting. *Not in a church. Maybe Spock could be the ring bearer? Will enough of Mummy's roses be blooming in September?*

Alarmed, she shook her head to dislodge these thoughts. She was not one who had dreamed of weddings and marriage; she had never played those wedding games as a child. She was of the age where a few of her friends had married, but marriage remained rather distant and abstract to her and she wouldn't have thought of it except that Clive had happened. Yes, she loved him extremely and couldn't imagine life without him. The problem was she needed to sort herself out first.

Spock had veered off the sidewalk to do his business. Afterward, when Poppy pulled out a plastic bag, Spock pretended he didn't see what she was doing. She was convinced he had chosen her for being slightly less crazy than most humans, but this fascination of hers, the *collecting*, was daily confirmation for him that humans teetered on the fringes of sanity.

Poppy kept a miniature garbage can beside the front steps in which to put these bags. (No danger of anyone stealing that can!) As she replaced the lid, the front door opened and there was barefoot Clive in T-shirt and sweatpants, hair standing on end.

"You're remembering I have that appointment today? You'll pick me up? At two?"

Poppy said, "I haven't forgotten." Which was true enough; she had thought of the appointment earlier even if she wasn't thinking about it right this second. Clive bent down and she stood on tiptoe to receive a scratchy kiss on her forehead. Spock licked Clive's toes and, after patting him, Clive went back in.

At the car—her Vista Cruiser station wagon, painted an anemic gold—she opened a back door for Spock. Then she opened her door and got in. The mug had made a steamy oval on the windshield.

The name Vista referred to the two "futuristic" rectangular slits of glass set into a slight elevation that interrupted the roofline. This had been her mother's car for about fifteen years and the mileage wasn't at all bad, since her mother only went to the A&P, the hairdresser, the big garden store, and her clubs. Once a year she drove to Maine. In Maine she didn't drive at all, as her house was in a fair-sized town that had everything a person could need within walking distance.

Her brother Price, the sibling to whom she was closest, had informed her that one or two siblings had muttered *unfair*, but no one denied that Poppy's life had blown the furthest off course and that none of them would have wanted the car anyway.

Poppy never bothered locking the car and she left the interior so untidy that even if there were a bag of gold coins somewhere, no one would be able to find it among the scatter of cans and cups, single gloves, broken plastic spoons, bent straws, candy wrappers, unspooling tape cassettes, and ripped paper bags filled with old books or clothes for Goodwill, where she always meant to stop but didn't. On the dashboard there was a banana skin that she and Clive referred to as "the science experiment." Somewhere loose under the front seat there was also a paperback of *Rich Man, Poor Man* with the cover torn off along with an equally mashed and stained paperback of travel essays by Edward Hoagland.

With the thought that it would be nicer for Clive if the front of the car were tidy, Poppy poked about for a plastic bag to stow the worst of the trash. Finding a roll of emergency paper towels squashed under the passenger seat, she poured water from Spock's bottle onto a couple of sheets and wiped the dust off the seat and the dash, carefully working around the black and wrinkled half-moon of the banana peel.

Spock was doing his thing on the back seat, which was to whirl around frantically until the large towel that Poppy shook out and tucked across the back seat at the end of each day was bunched up into a lumpy mass that he flopped onto with a satisfied grunt. She had tried leaving the towel untucked one time and Spock had jumped in the back and stood stock still, staring at the ruckled-up towel, utterly perturbed.

She put on her seat belt. The venerable station wagon *had* come equipped; Clive believed in seat belts, so Poppy had to do some serious excavating. Her mother had never used them.

Maneuvering with care out of the parking space, Poppy was on her way. First stop was Penelope's house in Society Hill.

A little before eight a.m., Poppy stood on the doormat of Irene Childress's handsome Georgian house, fumbling for the right key while Penelope barked with joyous fury on the other side of the door.

Irene, friendly with the visionary landscape architect who had campaigned for the resurrection of Society Hill, had been one of the very first to buy into the neighborhood and thus had had her pick of houses to choose from. Hers was an unusual Georgian-style house from the 1760s. The street front occupied two lots and the house was built sideways to the street, so that there was room for a large garden, not the usual postage stamp. There was a wide side alley too, where two cars could park one behind the other with plenty of space on either side. Irene rarely used her car and had put in automatic iron gates, leaving the outer parking spot open. She had filled her garden with tree peonies, variegated ground covers, some interesting sculptures, a small pond and fountain, and a slate terrace.

As Poppy inserted the correct key into the lock, Penelope began hurling herself against the door. Poppy slid inside, punched in the code to stop the bleat of the perimeter alarm, then bent down to let Penelope, who was bouncing and chuffing and wheezing around her ankles, lick her chin. While Poppy did not understand the appeal of their squashed-in noses, all the pugs she had met were decent little dogs. A little dim, but humble and friendly.

Irene Childress, Penelope's mistress, was Poppy's first and longest-running client—two years. Neither dog nor mistress was young; Irene was well into her eighties, and Penelope was past her first decade. For the time being, both seemed healthy enough, but to Poppy there was a precarious late-autumn mood.

While Penelope poked around in the garden, Poppy made her breakfast. Penelope was a lazy eater and Irene, concerned she wasn't eating enough, had her cook make special foods: mashed sweet potatoes and other dainties approved by the vet. Penelope remained a lazy eater. In Poppy's view the best cure for a lazy eater was another dog who *isn't* a lazy eater, but since that couldn't be arranged, Poppy had taken to leaving the breakfast food bowl out for only five minutes and Penelope had learned she had better eat some of her food right away. After a walk Poppy would offer the bowl again, and Penelope had learned to finish right up, for she knew her breakfast would disappear for good when Poppy left.

There was no sign of Irene, but that was normal. Irene had osteoarthritis and was stiff and sore in the joints when she first got up. She didn't like Poppy to see how difficult the stairs were for her in the morning, so she waited and came down while Poppy was out with Penelope. Poppy had once suggested that she might consider installing a stair lift, but Irene was scornful. By the afternoon Irene was positively spry and often took Penelope for amazingly long rambles.

Once outside, Penelope and Poppy went right to the car to invite Spock to come along, and Spock, as always, accepted, nimbly hopping down from the seat. He and Penelope got reacquainted, noses to ends, then nose to nose, after which Penelope did a sort of shimmy-shake to signal the end of the greeting ritual. She then trotted off, not without a fetching glance at Spock who, being Spock, appeared unmoved. Yet he liked Penelope or he wouldn't have gotten out of the car.

Taking their regular route, they walked north along Front Street as far as Chestnut, taking in a little of Independence Park before circling back through the extensive grounds of the controversial (as in plum ugly) Society Hill Towers. Penelope took her time, serious about sniffing and marking, but she was a considerate dog on the leash and the three of them ambled along contentedly.

In this neighborhood everything was swept and polished, the ivy trimmed and ironwork shiny. No trash on the sidewalks, no smashed windows or vomit or broken bottles. Even at the end of winter, when a bit of bedragglement is permitted, the area was spit-spot clean.

Poppy returned to the house to find a glamorously disheveled Irene, wrapped in a heavy dark blue satin robe over matching pajamas, standing on her doorstep. The satin was shot with silver starbursts and the neck and cuffs of the robe sported what was likely mink. Mr. Burns, her neighbor, impeccable in his gray pinstripe suit, had just stepped out of his own house, and was struck immobile by the sight of Irene in *deshabille*. Irene thought the Burnses dull, but they were good, kind people and Poppy had often urged Irene to cultivate them a little. Poppy guessed they were not unaware of Irene's disdain and were sporting enough to overlook her rudeness for the sake of neighborliness. The Burnses had a jovial Maltese named Ollie, but they also had a live-in housekeeper who normally walked him. Only when she was not available did they hire Poppy. Today, the reassuring sight of Poppy released Mr. Burns from his paralysis and he lifted his hat to Irene. Irene tossed her head, the silvery hair wavy and plentiful, acknowledging but not encouraging him.

"Poppy! At last! I'm brewing coffee." She turned to Mr. Burns, exclaiming, "Darling Mr. Burns, *such* a pleasure to see you, but I'm about to catch a chill, so I had better get inside."

In they swept.

"I can't stay, I have other clients waiting for me," Poppy said to forestall any attempt on Irene's part to rope her into the infinite number of "little jobs" Irene asked of her, such as changing a light bulb or moving a dresser to retrieve a dropped earring. Irene made a *moue,* an expression that went out with the blue satin house pajama; remorseful, Poppy gave her a quick hug, which she knew was all the physical contact Irene could handle—even then, her birdlike bones folded in protectively. No one, except doctors, touched her anymore.

"You have time for an espresso," Irene said firmly. She had left her cane just inside the door, not wanting to be seen in public using one, but as Poppy followed her into the kitchen, she noted Irene was leaning hard. Some joints must be hurting more than usual.

Coffee was brewing in an old stovetop espresso maker, an open can of Medaglio D'Oro nearby. Poppy's mother, under pressure from her children, had converted to buying fresh coffee beans, grinding as needed, and using a drip pot, but Irene stubbornly preferred the appallingly bitter brew of the enlightened coffee junkies of the previous generation.

Poppy sat down at the big round table. Visible among the clutter of pill bottles, salt and pepper shakers, a silver dish full of safety pins, stray buttons, and paper clips, was an unframed photograph that fascinated her. Not of Irene's three sons, as you might expect, but of two girls on the verge of becoming young women. Irene, in an unbecoming sailor-themed outfit and long blond braids, stands inelegantly beside a tiny wiry dark-haired girl in servant's black and white, her mass of black hair wound tightly into a bun, rebel strands poking out. Together they hold up a dog for the camera, some kind of spaniel; both girls wear expressions of pure delight.

On the back, in a rounded hand was written, "Me, Mathilde, and Pammy, 1913." Mathilde was the French-Canadian woman who had been Irene's lady's maid, housekeeper, and companion for over sixty years. Her death had precipitated the crisis that had brought Poppy into Irene's life.

From her own mother, Poppy had gleaned the basic facts. Irene's only sibling, a brother, had been killed in the First World War. Her mother had died of influenza in 1919. Her father had lived on, but went feral, spending most of the year at a remote Adirondack camp where he drank, hunted game, and played billiards with his friends. When he wasn't there, he was somewhere else shooting the local animals. He died of a fever on a trip to South America. Before that, he had become more attentive to his daughter after she married and began producing boys, three of them by 1932.

Irene displayed few family photographs, few photographs at all. On the bureau in her bedroom there was a rather sweet one of herself as a little girl with a big bow in her hair, sitting on a low stool at her mother's feet. Behind her mother's chair stands her father, and behind Irene stands her brother, looking proud in long pants. In the living room there were a few more photographs, one with her three sons under the age of ten, sitting together in three small chairs like the three bears, each chair the right size for each child. Two sons lived very far away, one in Hong Kong and the other in Los Angeles; the third was nearby out in the country, but as far as Poppy knew, he rarely came in to see his mother. Poppy had never met him.

Scattered about the living room were one photograph of each son with bride on their wedding day, but there were no pictures of her wedding or her husband (who had died soon after World War Two ended), or any of grandchildren. Much as she enjoyed Irene, it was likely, Poppy thought, that she had not been a lovable mother.

The only other photograph Poppy had ever seen on public display was also one of Irene and Mathilde and stood in the library, the room where Irene spent most of her time. That photograph had been taken probably about ten years after the first. The two were full-grown young women now, standing at the railing of an ocean liner, on a cloudy, windy day. Irene had on a long coat, probably blue, as that was "her" color, with the same sort of pale fur ruff at neck and wrists that she still favored, a cloche-type hat, and thick bobbed hair peeking out. Soberly dressed, but not unfashionable in a dark suit, Mathilde's hat was conservative and her hair was not bobbed. Pammy, now old and fat, sat at their feet, grinning, with her tongue hanging out.

The two were smiling for the camera, but there was no trace of their former youthful delight. Irene's smile was pure debutante; head slightly tilted back and to one side, it was obvious she knew how to show her "best" features. Mathilde's smile was stoic, and Poppy suspected she was feeling seasick. Poppy once removed the photograph from the frame to see if a date was written on the back, but there was nothing. Her guess was that the picture was taken on the honeymoon, and that Mr. Childress was behind the camera and that all three of them, and probably the dog too, already knew the marriage was not going to be much of a success.

As if divining Poppy's thoughts, Irene asked abruptly, "When is that darling boyfriend of yours going to propose?"

Poppy knew that for a moment her mouth made a perfect O of surprise. Irene was uncanny; she'd done this before, brought up some topic that Poppy was doing her best to ignore.

The espresso maker chose that moment to make the *gargle-whoosh* sound that meant the boiling water was heaving upward through the grounds, saving Poppy, at least temporarily, from having to answer.

Ever since Clive helped out once while Poppy had the flu, Irene has been fixated on him. Poppy had been too ill to think of warning him to start by saying "No" to her requests or he would be doomed. By the end of the week she had him clearing gutters, "taking a look" under sinks and into toilet workings, and fixing a leak in the fountain, making him both dirty and horrifically late to work. Irene was sturdily rich but she was also cheap.

Clive had grown up on a sort of a farm in Ohio, near a market town, and thus had many practical skills; his father was a newspaper editor, but he'd inherited the family farm, selling all but about thirty acres to a local dairy farmer, keeping the house, a woodlot and two fields. The kids had joined 4-H and they always had chickens, a couple of pigs, a milking cow, and several horses for family use. His mother liked to joke that the farm was a pretense for owning a tractor and truck, that buying the wood and hay would have been cheaper if you counted the labor and time spent repairing the machinery and barns, but she put up with it as she did adore her chickens.

After Poppy recovered, Clive had made her promise never to offer his services again. Since then he had visited Irene only infrequently and skittishly. That was one thing about Clive. He was endlessly kind and patient until he had had enough. Then he was adamant.

Irene turned from pouring the acidic stuff into tiny porcelain demitasse cups. "Never mind that," she said. "How is your writing going?" She was a writer. She had written three children's books inspired by her world travels, perhaps a trifle didactic but not bad, and had been a regular contributor to "style" magazines like *Town and Country* and still managed, about once a year, to publish something. She therefore considered herself a potential mentor, very irritating to Poppy although she did her best to hide her reaction.

"Slowly," Poppy decided to say.

Irene didn't know that Poppy had only said she was writing a novel in jest because of the remark her now ex-dissertation advisor had made. To her amazement this ploy proved to be a conversation stopper. She had *toyed* with the idea of writing a novel where James Boswell travels to the future and becomes a celebrated talk show host. She was convinced that Boswell *knew* in his bones that there was a future coming in which he would have been a free and healthy man and a celebrity just for being his irrepressible self. His contemporaries would have panicked at being transported into the future, but Poppy felt sure that after the initial shock, Boswell would have grasped the possibilities with gusto—especially after a visit to a doctor for his STDs (for surely he had all of them).

One of the only disagreements she had had with her brother Price in all the years since their father had left happened only a couple of months earlier, at Christmastime. In view of his surprising phone call a few months later, Poppy couldn't help but wonder if he hadn't already been practicing assertiveness.

They had gone for a walk at Valley Forge on a horrible windy day and in a fit of self-pity as they trudged around she had confided in him, at last, what the professor had said to her, something she had so far only told Clive. She then told him her idea for a novel, presenting it as a joke.

He had stunned her by urging her to consider trying it out, saying, "Sometimes the people who don't like you tell you things about yourself no one else will. You should go for it, Pops. It's a funny idea and your ideas have merit. I'll never forget acting in your plays, Pops. They were wild."

"A play isn't a novel," she had objected, "and I didn't *write*. None of you would memorize anything. I just told you who I wanted you to be and where I wanted the story to end up. Half the time you wouldn't even do that much for me. Rehearsals were a joke. The performances were ridiculous."

Price said sharply, "Poppy, can you accept a compliment?"

She was silent.

"Your plays are a clue, Poppy, about what you are good at. I never thought the PhD idea was right for you, if you want to know."

Now she was angry, "Thanks for your support."

"Did I ever say anything negative while you were pursuing that course?"

"No," she admitted, "but I just don't get it. What makes me unsuitable?"

"Do I really have to tell you? I think the man did you a favor."

"Right," Poppy said sarcastically, "look at me now, living up to my potential."

"Your life looks good to me. You have Clive. You love dogs. You'll figure out the rest as you go along."

"You have a great career, you are respected and making money. Isn't that what counts?" she said bitterly. "I have no idea what to do with the rest of my life. It's not a good feeling, Price."

"Don't envy me," Price said so harshly she didn't dare pursue the comment. He did that sometimes, just threw a blanket statement about himself, invariably negative, into a conversation.

Perhaps she hadn't been supposed to let matters stop there; perhaps she should have demanded an explanation.

Poppy gulped down Irene's coffee, bitter as wormwood and gall, as a pall of guilt settled around her for wishing to get away. All Irene wanted was to talk for a little while to a flesh-and-blood person about something more substantial than the weather, but Poppy had become stingy with Irene about allowing her private life to be a subject open for discussion. Yes, sure, she was paid to walk the dog, but with most of her clients you couldn't strip the job down to only the dog. The kinder thing would be to let Irene say her say, but she never knew when to stop. Poppy could imagine how her present course looked to Irene and her mother and many others and she could even concede that their concern was not entirely unwarranted but . . . she didn't know what exactly, only that nothing they could say would change that she had to figure out for herself what to do.

Spock chose that exact moment to look at her and then pointedly at the door. Quarter to nine. Time to get along to Fauna.

Poppy rinsed her cup and put it in the dishwasher. Penelope, tuckered out, was curled up in her sheepskin-lined bed; Poppy patted her head, which the little dog acknowledged by curling up tighter. Irene, pretending indifference to Poppy's intransigence, had picked up the newspaper.

Poppy almost blurted, "Probably Clive plans to propose today." *He will too,* she thought, *regardless of what the specialist says. He's waiting so that if the news is bad there will still be something to be happy about.*

She didn't *know* that, but suspected that was what Clive might be thinking.

At the car Poppy opened the door for Spock and then got in herself and began to back out into the street. She had come way too close to confiding in Irene, not because she had to but because Irene would love having a scoop.

The problem with Irene was not only the present neediness caused by Mathilde's death, but the fact that she was an exhausting person. But she was also generous and often very funny, more self-aware than one would suppose, given how vain, pigheaded, and opinionated she was. A few months after she had started walking Penelope, Irene had confided that until Mathilde's death she had never once in her life spent a night entirely alone; even before she was widowed. Mathilde had gone with her on all her trips, everywhere, even her honeymoon. She wasn't asking for pity, just explaining.

Over the past two years Irene had told her a lot about herself. Poppy found her childhood especially fascinating. Her own grandparents had all died when she was little. Irene was the first person she'd gotten to know since she was old enough to care who had grown up before the First World War. Born in the late 1890s into a very well-off family, Irene had a childhood that might appear romantic and idyllic. Besides their town house in the city and a big place in the country, the family had a rustic camp in the Adirondacks and another house on the North Shore of Massachusetts. Irene's brother, ten years older, was a stranger to her. At the age of seven he was sent to boarding school and after that he never lived at home for more than a few weeks at a time again, as he was always going to camps, or to visit friends, or to go out West to work at a dude ranch or something enviably fun.

Irene's parents were essentially nomadic, interspersing their frequent moves among their own houses with long trips abroad. Irene followed her parents from place to place, first with nannies and then governesses, most of whom were kindly and did their best to be decent company and to teach her what they could. At the camp she learned to hunt and fish. Nearer to home she learned to ride sidesaddle and go fox hunting. When on the North Shore, she sailed and did her best with tennis and golf. From governesses and the endless travel, she learned to read and speak French and Italian fluently and enough German to get by. On rainy days she read freely in her parents' libraries, kept up-to-date by a secretary for show as neither parent was much of a reader.

Often Irene was left with staff for months on end while her parents went on trips deemed too dangerous for a child, say, floating down the Nile in a barge or going to Japan because Papa had business interests and the Emperor had invited him or India so Papa could hunt tigers and her mother could buy silks. Irene had kept none of her father's trophies, but evidence of her mother's love of exquisite textiles was everywhere in the house. When Irene turned fifteen, her parents decided she was through with governesses. She would attend a finishing school in Switzerland for a year and when she returned she would be given her own lady's maid to dress her hair and look after her as she prepared to be a debutante.

Enter Mathilde.

Poppy had quickly become curious about Mathilde, but refrained, at first, from asking in case talking about her would upset Irene.

One morning Irene came upon Poppy studying the photograph in the kitchen.

"That photograph was taken in 1913," she said. "It was the first day I realized that my life had changed for the better. At long last I had a friend I wouldn't have to leave behind."

As Irene explained, Poppy understood that from the age of fifteen until Mathilde died, *this* was the person with whom Irene had shared her life.

1913. One of those dates that gives a thoughtful person the shivers.

"If you look closely at the picture, you'll see that one of Pammy's front paws is bandaged."

Poppy looked more closely. She hadn't noticed.

"Mattie had been at our house for about four months," Irene said. "I was almost sixteen, the year when most girls put up their hair. This was also the year when the birthday parties changed. Instead of magicians and clowns and pony rides, they began to happen in the late afternoon and included dancing, which meant boys and musicians and dressing up. Time for me to prepare for my debut.

"When I returned from the finishing school, Mattie was already at the house, learning her job. She had known nothing about being a lady's maid, but my mother hired her because she could sew beautifully, and my mother figured if she could do that she could learn all the rest. She was taught by my mother's maid, an Irishwoman, how to dress hair and iron even the most delicate laces, to pack clothes so they wouldn't wrinkle, to take stains off of cloth shoes, and all the thousand tasks a lady's maid undertakes so that the lady is free to go to teas, wander about gardens, and spend hours staring out the window. I spoke French well, but she was Québecois, and her accent and idioms were so different that we could barely communicate at first." Irene sighed. "I hated it. Mattie was always scurrying about tidying up after me and she was so small and quick and quiet, I felt spied on. Also she was always scowling, which unnerved me. I thought she hated me. Poor Mattie, she was just trying to be useful and keep her job. And the scowling? She told me later, she was trying not to cry. I was so upset when she told me that. I knew I hadn't done anything spiteful or cruel, you understand, but I had done all I could to pretend she didn't exist. I never gave her feelings a thought.

"Then one day, Pammy, my little dog, about two years old, got a long thorn in her paw and it was Mattie who saved the day, who got the splinter right out and knew exactly how to clean and bandage such a deep wound. My father happened to be about taking pictures of his new tennis court, and he made us stand still while he took that picture. From then on we were . . ." Irene stopped with a mischievous smile, "in cahoots. I lost my copy of that photograph along the way, but Mattie kept this one on her own dresser."

Irene's blue eyes, normally very clear, went sort of opaque whenever she talked about Mathilde. "After I married, I told Mattie many times that she was free to go if she wished, I would make sure she would have enough income to be independent, to start a dressmaking business of her own if she liked, but she said she liked her life with me and was no longer angry with her family for selling her off. If she hadn't left home, she always said, she would probably have died young of hard work or in childbirth, the fate of two of her four sisters. Once a year, after I was married, I sent her off to see them all, loaded up with gifts. As far as they were concerned, she was the rich aunt who had done well in 'L'Amerique.'"

At the end of one installment of their story, Irene tossed her head so that Poppy knew she was about to say something outrageous.

Fixing her still extraordinary violet-blue eyes on Poppy she said puckishly, "I suppose today someone writing a biography about me would feel obliged to poke and pry for signs that we were lesbian lovers, but they would be wasting their time."

Poppy was right about the photograph upstairs. Irene's new husband had been looking through the viewfinder on their honeymoon trip. The marriage was not happy, but it was civil as they ignored one another after they had done their duty and had three sons. In 1947 he died and conveniently left her a fortune. Irene had never remarried and over time she achieved *grande dame* status in Philadelphia society and was to be seen at every fund-raising gala or any opening of new dance, art, music, or theater, the more avant-garde the better. She lobbied hard for legalizing bare breasts in "artistic" productions and for theaters to feature black actors, as Philadelphia was one of those prudish and quietly racist cities that lagged far behind the tidal wave of loosening inhibitions and taboos elsewhere. She'd told Poppy once that she had her first orgasm sliding down a bannister, but still had no idea until she took on a lover that this was something that should happen during sex! "When I found out," she said, "I felt so *cheated.*"

Washington Square was close enough to walk to but Poppy didn't feel comfortable asking Irene if she could leave the car for an extra hour. Especially since Millicent Steingarten, Fauna's mistress, had arranged for Poppy to park in the garage under her apartment building. The space was anything but ideal, but Poppy felt obliged after the trouble Millicent had taken.

To walk around with Fauna was to be in the limelight. She was the dog equivalent of a Botticelli maiden. People's eyes would glaze over at the sight of her; they would be in danger of stepping in front of a bus as they tried to get one last glimpse. A two-year-old Russian wolfhound, she was more than elegant, she was a work of art. Poppy found Fauna's self-awareness almost eerie, as if she was cognizant of the effect she had on people and of the responsibilities that go with being beautiful and admired. Her patience and graciousness with her admirers was without limit.

Fauna lived in a stately apartment building on Washington Square. Poppy walked her on most weekday mornings, unless Millicent had the day off. Millicent took Fauna down to the park first thing before leaving for work and always came home by four p.m. to spend time with her. When she couldn't get home, which was often, with late lessons, interviews, auditions, and concerts, Poppy came back.

Millicent, who was around sixty, taught voice at the Curtis Institute. She sang beautifully herself (mezzo soprano), but suffered from an insurmountable debilitating performance anxiety that had come on in her early thirties that she had never fully overcome. She could only sing spontaneously and informally for a very small audience in a private home. This handicap had stymied her performing career but her singing was legendary. Those who had had the good fortune to hear her, Irene said, boasted dreadfully, but not without reason. Millicent was a superb teacher and beloved by all. Her specialty was lieder, German love songs, apple blossoms and so forth. Out of respect for Millicent, Poppy had given lieder a listen, but could not see the appeal.

Millicent was a dog owner without fault but Fauna was only two and needed much more exercise than Millicent could give her, which is where Poppy came in.

In the garage Poppy had been assigned a space in the area reserved for repair men and deliveries, unfortunately beside a support column with barely room for a car as large as the Vista Cruiser to squeeze into. If the space beside was occupied, she could not get in or out unless she had backed into the space at a slight angle. Clive could, no doubt, explain the physics of why it worked in this direction but not the other.

Spock, knowing where they were going, would ride in the front passenger seat and then clamber out with Poppy, so anxious was he not to be left behind. At first she had taken him up to Fauna's floor with her, but one thing Spock could not handle was elevators. Being Spock he got in uncomplainingly, then trembled and drooled all the way up and down. Henry, the door man, had noticed Spock's misery and had said, "Leave her boyfriend with me while you get the princess. No problem."

Poppy agreed to this and told Spock to sit and stay beside Henry at his desk. After a time she realized that Henry and Spock were conspiring. When she returned Spock might be sitting, all right, but on the opposite side of the desk from where she had left him. She pretended not to notice. Spock did have that sly, secretive side and that was how he had come to her after all.

As she opened the door to the flat, Fauna jumped gracefully off the couch, her plumed tail waving slowly, and came over to give Poppy's extended fingers the lightest and most delicate of licks. One didn't have to bend over at all to pat her head, which she offered to Poppy, leaning a little against her hip.

"Ready?" Poppy asked her.

Where most other dogs this young would be leaping up and slavering with joy, Fauna only danced, her nails clattering musically on the marble in the foyer. Poppy took the leash from a hook under the mirror and snapped it onto her collar.

During the walk Spock, who was besotted with Fauna, trotted alongside occasionally glancing at the other dog's profile, waving his tail as elegantly as he could. The little glances were both to take in Fauna's beauty and to see, Poppy always felt, if Fauna was noticing *him*. When she did happen to return the glance, Poppy could see Spock shiver with delight.

Fauna's walk was brisk, a half-hour at something close to a jog, more when there was time. Near the end of their loop, while they were crossing Independence Park, Poppy had discovered a private place, walled in on three sides by brick with no windows and a perfect lawn, an oval, about the length and width (at the center) of a tennis court. The fourth side was fenced by a massive hedge with a break in it for what her mother called a "moon gate." As the garden was raised about two feet above the rest of the grounds and had a thick hedge of evergreens, passersby could not see in unless they walked up the three steps to the moon gate. No one ever did.

This was the sort of gate that led one to believe in magic portals through which you walked into other worlds. No one had ever entered when Poppy was there. No one else ever appeared to even notice the garden's existence. Someone must have been tending the area because the lawn was always luxuriously verdant, and well mowed. The shrubbery, too, was pruned and the ground underneath weeded and mulched. The only shrubs were azaleas and rhododendrons and a row of cedars across the open side, massed so thickly that the only gap through which you could see was the gate.

The garden looked so private that Poppy had hesitated, at first, to go in, but there were no signs saying to keep out and the gate was never locked. After a few tentative visits, Poppy had realized that in this space she could safely let Fauna run free. After that, she stopped here every day.

One of Poppy's firmly held convictions was that every dog should have the opportunity to roll around in grass or dirt or snow every day. As soon as Poppy let Fauna off the leash she would always fling herself into the luscious grass (or snow, in winter).

After the rolling, Fauna would allow herself a few minutes of what can only be described as "crazy dog," where she would careen around the garden like a mad thing. Spock generally stood in the middle of the oval watching Fauna adoringly as she ran circles and figure eights around him, moving like witchlight as if gravity had no hold over her. When she was through, she would hurl herself down near him, panting, her tongue lolling.

Eventually Fauna would rise and wander off with a few covert glances at Poppy and Spock, who would look the other way as she ducked into the rhododendrons. After Fauna's return, Poppy would, nonchalantly, retrieve the item while Fauna would now be the one looking the other way, or meditatively licking her paw, at any rate, intently pretending not to know what Poppy was doing.

Fauna, like Spock, was hyperaware of human social cues. Humans went into bathrooms alone. Fauna, too, was discreet beyond the norm. Poppy had little doubt that the more intelligent the dog, the more they observed and imitated human behaviors and tried them out—adopting the ones that worked, which included simple practical jokes, expressing shame, and declaring undying love. Spock even exhibited different behaviors in different settings, as if he knew that a dirty dog in the city was more problematic than a dirty dog in the country. In town, he avoided puddles, in the country he splashed through them, even lay down in them sometimes, the muddier the better.

Upon their return Poppy would leave Spock with Henry, while she took Fauna up to the flat, where she would thoroughly wipe off the greenish tint of grass from paws and tummy on the fresh towel Millicent left every day for that purpose in the vestibule.

After checking that the water bowl was fresh and full and placing the towel in the laundry room, Poppy would sometimes pause to absorb the atmosphere of Millicent's flat. Poppy couldn't explain the emotion the flat evoked in her. The furnishings spoke of values, culture, and a history in some ways familiar, in others completely different from her own. The antiques were all from *Mitteleuropa*: a Biedermeyer cabinet here, an ormolu gilded clock there, Meissen porcelain figures ranged on shelves, a small Bosendorfer grand piano painted ivory, a color that Poppy would normally scoff at but here, amongst all the gold gilt, yellow, and ivory with tiny splashes of green or red, the effect was soothing and pleasing; Poppy felt rough and a little uncultured, a feeling she rarely had.

As well as being the flat of someone moderately successful, it was the home of a person who had never married or had children. Shared homes, unless one person is entirely passive about decor, generally have a schizophrenic quality from the push and pull of different ideas about comfort and aesthetics. Not so here. Here, everything was as Millicent wished and Fauna was exactly the right companion to bring the whole ensemble to life. There was nothing contrived. The flat had a beguiling warmth and comfort, if perhaps too quiet with only the tick of the clock. When Millicent was home, there was always music playing.

Today she did not linger. Always before leaving Poppy would offer a parting biscuit, which Fauna would gently take from her fingers over to "her" couch where she would begin to crunch her treat.

It was not quite ten o'clock in the morning when Poppy returned to the parking garage to find the Vista Cruiser nearly parked in by a van so huge that she would have to pull out inch by inch.

Her next clients, the dog and the owners, were her least favorites. The Balderstons managed to be simultaneously ghastly and pitiable. Moreover they were barely acceptable as dog owners. Like many supremely difficult people, they had a weird allure to Poppy and they provided more anecdotal material than any of her other clients. Clive was most likely, at the end of the day, to ask if there were any new Balderston horrors to share. Often there were.

They paid ridiculously well. They had to.

The Balderstons lived in a fine house on Delancey, a short walk from Rittenhouse Square. All she knew, vaguely, was that Mr. B had made loads of money in real estate. Certainly, they had enough to fling around. Mrs. B could never settle on a decor, which meant that the house was in a perpetual turmoil of workers painting, replacing curtains, carpets, flooring, and furniture. Right now Mrs. B was shifting fabrics from primary colors to chintz, which was back in favor.

From the first, Poppy had recognized in the Balderstons traces of what Henry James might have called a hollowness at the core. Nothing seemed to go deeper than a coat of nail polish. Indeed, one had the sense that this thin coating covered something best left unseen, or perhaps a void. They read nothing; they knew almost nothing about art or music or culture, or food, or animals or . . . much of anything as far as Poppy could tell. That they could be aliens from outer space had crossed her mind. Like Gatsby, their accents revealed nothing so they didn't seem to be *from* anywhere, and she guessed that their true names had been abandoned. Also like Gatsby, they had a fixed notion that there existed an elite to aspire to, unaware that even if once upon a time there had been such an elite, abundant new money and new values were rapidly rendering the concept obsolete. The stupendously wealthy were as "in" as anyone could be.

Whatever the source of their fortune, they had "retired" to Center City Philadelphia convinced that somewhere was a "society" that would take them in if they got themselves onto various museum boards. Their ambitions made Poppy cringe but they also made her feel ashamed of herself, as she knew that one reason they paid her so generously and gave her the perks they did was that they believed she was "the real thing," Old Philadelphia, Quaker roots, Social Register and all. If even their dog-walker was posh, this might help them.

Both Balderstons used the word "lifestyle" constantly. They had stacks of magazines, from *Architectural Digest* and *House Beautiful* to the lavish *English Homes & Gardens* to *Interior Design,* and they believed implicitly that by spending money on the right accessories and activities, they would acquire social standing.

After one conversation, Poppy had realized that Mrs. B thought that there were still rules about what a person should wear for particular activities. She had asked Poppy what sort of shoes one wore on a motorboat and if that was different from the shoes you would wear on a sailboat. Poppy answered honestly saying, "No. You just wear shoes that won't hurt the decks and will help keep you from sliding off if the boat tips." Mrs. B. looked so disappointed that Poppy considered making something up, like blue for sailboats, red for motorboats. Another time Mrs. B asked about what kind of hat her mother wore to the Devon Horse Show, apparently confusing the event with Ascot. Again Poppy was tempted to make something up, but she opted for the truth: "My mother doesn't wear anything on her head unless it's raining or cold, in which case she keeps these folding plastic hats in her raincoat pocket. Her winter hat is even worse, a purple one with a green pompom that one of my sisters knitted."

Telling Mrs. Balderston the truth, however, was a waste of time. When her employer, who slightly resembled a troll, said, "I'm thinking white, with a wide brim," Poppy had to hide her delight at the remark. Something to tell Clive tonight.

Poppy was sure that her mother's daily life could not be described as a lifestyle. Maybe she had started out with one: there was a photograph of her looking serenely gorgeous at a post-party party at The Stork Club (her father, then impossibly good-looking, at her side with a cigarette in hand), for example, and another one with her and Daddy dressed up to go to the wedding of some Polish prince. Her mother had been asked if she'd like to try modeling sports clothes once, when she was shopping for camping gear at Abercrombie and Fitch.

Poppy's mother did live in a wonderful large house on the Main Line that she had bought with Poppy's father twenty-six years ago. It was full of furniture she had mostly inherited, so there were oil portraits of genuine ancestors, and epergnes and Willow pattern china so old it had no markings and a silver filigee Victorian tea service that was a nightmare to polish. Poppy's father's family, Massachusetts Puritans, had been whalers and merchants and when he left for good he left many possessions behind, such as a cabinet full of oddities like thumb-size tea cups painted with one-hair brushes, carved ivory Buddhas, and venetian blown-glass figures that glowed like emeralds and sapphires in the light.

Yet there was nothing in her mother's *actual* daily life that had one iota of glamor, which Poppy assumed was a lifestyle requirement. Left with six children, ranging from age two to sixteen, their mother, after a period of severe depression, had discovered that she rather liked being independent. She had finished her BA at the University of Pennsylvania, then worked in admissions at Bryn Mawr College for a few years. More recently, after getting an MSW at Villanova, she was tutoring children for an organization that helped families in crisis. She retained all of her childhood friends, even those now living far away. A shocking number, almost all of whom Poppy loved, were divorced or widowed.

Now that her children were all close to being grown up, Mummy had her roses and her garden club, the Acme, and her book club, in that order of importance. She had tickets to the orchestra for the same pair of seats she had sat in since she used to go with her own mother. Poppy wasn't keen on classical music, generally, but Clive loved it and went with her mother frequently. Her mother also went faithfully to every new show at the art museum, and subscribed to theater seasons and went to the movies often, always with a friend or two. If she flew somewhere, she went coach. The point is, her mother saw the same old people, did the same activities every day, wore clothing and shoes she'd had for decades. She wore no makeup, beyond a bit of lipstick.

At home, her mother pottered about her garden looking less like a former debutante and more like a Chekhov sister thirty years on, in a floppy hat, baggy jeans or ancient madras shorts, and shapeless L. L. Bean tops. When the day was very hot, sometimes her mother just wore an old bathing suit with a long-tailed button-down shirt, sleeves rolled up.

Her mother might, if she had company, get out the best china or even the silver but for daily use it was mugs and tea bags and stainless. Her mother's sheets, from her trousseau, were linen and monogrammed; everyone else in the house slept on plain cotton bought at the white sales at Strawbridge's, much mended and patched either by herself or Sybil until demoted to cleaning rags.

Oh, her mother's social life was certainly *exclusive*, meaning she had a very small circle of like-minded friends. Any glamor had been abandoned along with gloves and petticoats in the 1960s, after Poppy's father took LSD, started smoking pot, and then went off to India with a graduate student (not the one he later married).

Interestingly, Poppy thought that Boswell, even though he was from a "good" Scottish family, had social delusions in common with the Balderstons. When he arrived in London, he was already convinced that the "real" aristocrats were living lives of enviable glamor and he became obsessed with joining a particular English regiment which, he was sure, would give him entry into that exalted society. Everyone who knew him knew his ambition to be a soldier was unrealistic, and the notion that the aristocrats would embrace him if he became one, ridiculous. He was not military material, would likely be insubordinate almost immediately, and would surely disgrace himself and whoever had sponsored him, before long. She had puzzled over the fact that his quasi-patron, Lord Eglinton, let Boswell hope for much longer than he should have, that he would help him in his quest. Poppy had originally assumed that it could be maliciousness or at least carelessness, but now she wondered if Eglinton might have felt as she did about the Balderstons, that telling the truth to Boswell would have been embarrassing, awkward, and possibly damaging to an already unstable person. It is possible that Eglinton was doing all he could to let a volatile friend down gently.

The Balderstons' acquisition of a dog was harder to theorize about. They were clearly not dog people. Poppy's best guess was that Mrs. Balderston had seen a King Charles spaniel lying on a mat in front of a fireplace in a catalog or magazine and thought, *I must have one of those*, the way you might choose a bathmat. Had Poppy liked Horatio better she would have considered arranging to have him kidnapped, but Horatio's problems defeated even Poppy's patience and love for dogs; she didn't want Horatio (not that she would do anything so treacherous to Spock or Clive) but there was no one she could think of on whom she could inflict him.

At the very least, Poppy was glad that the Balderstons weren't actively mean to Horatio; he was an accessory, and as such they never would harm or injure him in any way. He was part of their "lifestyle," but he was neither loved nor needed, and he was a mess.

Sadly, Horatio couldn't even perform his role as accessory very often as he suffered from a variety of skin ailments and was often attired in a plastic collar. Happily for Horatio, nothing but nothing embarrassed him. He was a leg-humper, a crotch-sniffer, a poop-eater, and he yanked one about mercilessly on the leash. At the park he would sometimes plop down firmly in the middle of the path and begin working over, with obvious relish, some unspeakable part of his anatomy. He barked hysterically at everything: toddlers, squirrels, and other dogs, always straining and making death-rattle choking sounds on the leash that made people glare at Poppy.

Spock would not leave the car for Horatio. As far as he was concerned Horatio was a smell so foul that even a dog couldn't work up any enthusiasm. Spock would never have bitten Horatio, but at a look from Spock, Horatio widdled and fell over on his back whimpering. Poppy wanted to feel pity for him, he as much as every dog merited attention and affection, but alas, for Horatio, the harder you tried the more you failed.

On the weekends, Mrs. B walked Horatio. Poppy knew from Lorena that Mrs. B had a special outfit for these outings: special shoes, special dog-walking coat, special gloves, special hat. There was even a special matching leash and collar that

Poppy wasn't to use. On Saturday and Sunday mornings, Mrs. B supposedly walked decorously around the park with her dog, being "seen" as a loving dog owner. Poppy couldn't imagine how this scenario could possibly be decorous or loving, given how badly behaved Horatio was.

"She don't even pick up his, you know?" Lorena had said. "She walks on like nothin' came out of his rear." Poppy knew this for the truth as Horatio liked to poop in the same corner and on Mondays there were always two new poops (which Poppy picked up, wondering if Mrs. Balderston ever wondered how the poops magically went away).

There were perks. Twice, the Balderstons had hired Poppy to drive Horatio and their car, a handsome convertible Mercedes, to and from their winter home on Siesta Key in Sarasota, as Mrs. B had a horror at the idea of a dog put in the baggage hold. (This was a point in her favor, Poppy felt.) Naturally, Clive came along to help with the driving and the Balderstons paid for their flights, as well as graciously offering them a week in their guest house in both December and in March.

The first night after they arrived in Florida, the Balderstons always had them over for awkward cocktails, but for the remainder, they went their own ways, agreeable to everyone. Poppy noted that the Balderstons were happier and more at home in Florida, and wondered why they didn't stay there. In a landscape of transients with money, they fit in well.

The Balderstons leased five permanent parking spaces in an open lot about two blocks away, two for themselves, one for her use, and the rest for the endless parade of tradesmen. Poppy drove in, waving at the proprietor, Val, then cranked open the windows, and left Spock curled up on his lumpy towel. He opened one eye and gave her a look that meant *better you than me.*

As Poppy let herself in, Horatio came skittering out of the back of the house, barking. When he saw her, he widdled on the black and white tiles in the foyer.

Horatio was not wearing his collar, which meant the Balderstons were not at home. Lorena couldn't abide the collar and took it off the minute the Balderstons went out and kept him in her sights, not hard since the two of them spent most of their time in the kitchen. Besides cooking, Lorena's duties consisted of answering the phone, letting the workmen in and out and keeping an eye on them, doing local shopping, and being company for Horatio. Because of all the dust and mess, she'd put her foot down about cleaning and now the Balderstons hired a team who could keep up with the constant renovations. If she had to leave Horatio, Lorena put the collar back on, but the rest of the time the squirt bottle was tucked into her apron, cowboy-style so she could paste him if he started chewing or scratching at himself. Every time Horatio would jump into the air as if electrocuted and then look left and right indignantly, his ears flapping, while Lorena cackled gleefully. He never figured out where the water was coming from, never suspected Lorena.

Like Poppy, Lorena was overpaid or she would not have been there.

Lorena appeared behind Horatio. "I been waiting for you to get in. Your husband says call him at work, right away. He made it sound real urgent." She had decided that because they lived together Poppy and Clive were married and Poppy did not bother protesting although the lack of a wedding band gave it away.

They were only supposed to use the phone in the kitchen so Poppy and Lorena made their way down the long narrow hall. Surprisingly, the kitchen had never been remodeled and was a period piece of the 1940s, reddish brown and white linoleum tiles and minimal counter space as well as anomalies such as the immense stainless steel refrigerator. Given how intently Mrs. B studied those architecture magazines it was mystifying that she did not seem to get that today's kitchen was the centerpiece of a home. Well, maybe it was understandable, why do over a kitchen when you had no intention of spending any time in it yourself, so it would be primarily for the benefit of your cook? If her dream was to be featured in one of those magazines, she'd have to get to the kitchen. Poppy expected that her interior designer tried to tell her and met with the same wall she had about the hats.

Lorena's primary job was to cook up and freeze what were essentially home-made TV dinners; she made plain fare, stews, chicken with biscuits, and the like and froze them in those compartmented container trays. If the Balderstons were home for lunch she fed them various simple soups (cooked from scratch and kept frozen and ready) with toast and salad. Because they ate out so often and so lavishly, both Balderstons vigilantly watched their weight and ate simply at home. They were rigorous in pursuit of their dream.

When they were not going out, Lorena was told to take the pre-made dinners upstairs to thaw. In their private "den" room, there was a mini-kitchen with a microwave (Poppy had never gone upstairs). Lorena said they sat on two loungers and ate off of hospital-style tables while watching television. They piled their empties in the sink of the mini-kitchen for Lorena to deal with the next day or after the weekend. For breakfast Mrs. B ate yogurt out of the container from the mini-fridge upstairs and Mr. B went out somewhere for his. They almost never set foot in the kitchen.

While Lorena didn't care for Horatio any more than Poppy did, she also worried about his well-being over the weekends, even if he never seemed worse for the wear on Mondays. She left prepared meals for Horatio in carefully labeled bowls, "Sat a.m." and so forth. She filled two water bowls full. Horatio spent the weekends in the kitchen, and as far as Lorena knew, the only time Mr. or Mrs. B came into the main kitchen was to feed Horatio, get a meal out of the freezer, or to take him out. On Mondays there was always widdle somewhere but rarely poop.

Lorena's comment was, "I seen dogs treated worse," which Poppy knew to be true. So had she.

Poppy picked up the receiver of the wall phone, the old kind with a rotary dial and a short cord, and dialed Clive's work number. If he were involved in a project he was capable of tuning out a ringing telephone but after only three rings he picked up.

"Farmer here," he said absently.

Lorena pretended to be bustling around, but Poppy could feel her ears straining to find out what could be so important that her husband had tracked her down here.

"It's me. Calling you back."

"Hi darling," Clive said. "I'm sorry to bother you, but Price just called from Chicago, in between flights. He gets in around 1:30 and he was wondering if you could pick him up and take him out to your Mom's later. I told him we had this appointment. I think he thinks it's some kind of counseling. I didn't explain."

"Oh boy," Poppy said. "Are you okay about this? Are you thinking what I'm thinking?"

A month ago Poppy's brother Price had called them. After apologizing for using the phone for momentous news, he told Poppy that she was the first person he was telling that he was gay, that he had decided to officially come out, but was going to go slowly, first telling his siblings and closest friends whose support he was sure of having. When he was feeling more used to the idea, he would tell their mother and probably their father.

Poppy was floored, and even though she had (she hoped) said what one is supposed to, she was all the while prickling with shock—not because her brother was gay, but because she had had no idea whatsoever! The possibility had never entered her mind, though once stated it was instantly *obvious*. How could she have been so unaware? She who was supposedly closer to him than anyone? To her everlasting shame she had even, in the moment before he told her, thought he might be announcing his engagement to someone, a woman. He was secretive, but she had never imagined that he was *this* secretive.

He had always had close women friends, friendships that teetered on the edge of becoming something more . . . usually they didn't, or if they did, only briefly. Price was notoriously fussy about his friendships and that was one reason she had never considered that he might be gay; she assumed he would hold out for the right woman.

Fine. Yes. But. If she had been paying attention, maybe she should have wondered. If anyone in her family considered the possibility, she should have. How much might she have failed Price by being so dense?

Clive brought Poppy back to the present, saying, "Yeah, he's going to make it official and tell your Mom."

"Would it be better for you if I took him to Suburban Station and put him on the Paoli Local?" Poppy asked.

Clive made a noise that she knew was his way of admitting he would have preferred to do that, but then he said, "How can we say no? I just told him you'd pick him up and we'd figure it out. The weather's good, his plane's not delayed."

"But, what about the test results?" Clive had decided no one but Poppy should know about the test. "We'll have to tell Price what it's about."

"Well, if he can come out, I can come clean."

Poppy held the phone, her eyes prickling. Was this loyalty to a fault on the day you might learn you had a serious heart defect? Yes and no. Both Price and her mother would be good people to be with if the news was bad.

"All right," Poppy said, "if I have any kind of problem picking him up, I'll find a phone and call you or the doctor's office. If I'm *not* there at the time you need to get moving, just go, and I'll get to the hospital one way or the other." They said their goodbyes.

As Poppy hurried out with Horatio the day felt entirely different. The light was harsher, edges were more distinct, and the breeze cooler. She took Horatio on his usual route at a trot, which he didn't appreciate. When they got to the square he simply refused to move fast, snuffling at every candy wrapper, every dropped twig. Some child had left a fuzzy stuffed animal, a rabbit, on the ground and Horatio, after sniffing, started to hump it. People were staring. 10:45 a.m. Time to go.

Ten minutes later Poppy was whisking down Kelly Drive beside the Schuylkill River en route to Mount Airy and her most distant client, Rosalie Miller. Midmorning on a weekday, she had the road to herself. The light through the leafless trees was very bright, flags snapped in front of the boathouses, and the rowers were out preparing for the big regatta only a month away, battling the windy chop. The apple trees were not quite in bloom, but the grass was greening.

Rosalie was about as pleasant a person as you could dream up. Somewhere in her fifties, she was one of those teachers whom students naturally love and respect and who make teaching look like an easy and enviable career. Her house, a sweet Arts and Crafts bungalow, was tucked behind a larger house and overlooked Wissahickon Park. Inside, her house was possibly even more appealing. Bookshelves climbed the walls up three sides of the open-to-the-rafters living room, where a mezzanine ranged around two sides and featured more bookshelves plus a reading nook in an alcove that opened onto a balcony. The living room was furnished comfortably, with both reading and sociability in mind. The window seats had plenty of plump cushions and invited daylight reading; there were deep velvety chairs and well-placed lamps for nighttime. Kitchen, bathroom, bedrooms, were all pleasant afterthoughts: functional, plain, and comfortable. Knick-knacks given to her by students were scattered around among good watercolors, mostly landscapes featuring water and trees. This was a dream house made real.

Rosalie would be a temporary client, Poppy hoped. A double mastectomy and chemo had made impossible walking her two corgis enough to keep them from getting fat. Rosalie had a zillion devoted friends, but she had decided they were doing too much for her already, cooking and shopping and driving her about, so she hired Poppy, having heard of her in some roundabout way. Most of Poppy's clients were referred through Poppy's mother or Irene, but this referral came through a former roommate of hers, presently teaching science at the school where Rosalie had taught English for decades.

When Poppy pulled up she was delighted to see Rosalie outside, clad in a long fuzzy cardigan, scarf, and wide-brimmed hat, standing behind the low stone wall of her garden, a trowel in hand. Bliss and Chutney started barking and running in protective circles around Rosalie the moment Poppy opened her car door. Three months had passed and soon there would come a day when Rosalie would say, "I think I can do the walking myself," and Poppy had mixed feelings. She'd be happy for Rosalie, but being paid to walk two very amusing dogs in the Wissahickon, not to mention Rosalie herself, made this a most relaxing stop. There would be no reason she couldn't come out now and then to visit, but Rosalie had so many loving friends, she knew she wouldn't.

Like Millicent, Rosalie had never married, and yet her style couldn't have been more different from Millicent's cool elegance; Rosalie was plump (a little less so now), cheerful with a gleeful laugh. Rosalie's sharp blue eyes missed nothing, nor did her ears; she could focus suddenly on you like a raptor, making you question the wisdom of whatever you had just said. Poppy had decided that Rosalie was part Mrs. Piggle-Wiggle, part adult Pippi Longstocking, and the rest a bona fide Elizabeth Bennett who had decided being Mrs. Darcy was too much bother. Describing to Clive how much she liked Rosalie, he had surprised Poppy by saying, "Sounds like she's your only happy client."

This was true, she realized: even with Millicent, there was a slight emotional drain, an underlying sadness that neither her work nor her dog could fill.

Spock had jumped out with her, for he would not miss a walk in the Wissahickon. He waited outside the garden while Poppy went to get the leashes, which were hung on a hook in the covered entryway. The circling corgis saw the leashes and abandoned Rosalie, who laughed at them. Rosalie invited her to come in for tea after, and Poppy regretfully explained she had to get back into town to pick up her brother at the airport.

Poppy and the three dogs headed for the path to the bridge across the creek to Forbidden Drive. Spock stayed close. He couldn't make up his mind about the corgis; they insisted on frolicking and teasing and would not tolerate his stuffy aloofness. Once Poppy let Bliss off the leash she would nip at Spock's heels, ducking and rolling over, and racing off in an unexpected direction before he could even turn around to see where she was. He couldn't win, and he eventually forgot his dignity and gave chase, first annoyed, then for fun. They were good for him, Poppy thought.

The route Poppy took today led to a promontory where a group of big flat stones lay high above and the creek took a sharp turn toward the Schuylkill. There were places even in as heavily used a park as this one where the earlier, native presence yet hovered, and this was one. This was a sacred place and these rocks were kept clean, no broken glass or trash about, and from time to time she would find a sprinkling of tobacco or cornmeal. When she had the time she sat awhile and invariably a sense of quietude came over her.

Even today, when this could be no more than a token stop, Poppy sat down anyway. The dogs, used to this and knowing that she kept biscuits in her pockets, came and sat or lay down beside her, lifting their noses to smell whatever was on offer while Poppy looked at the strangely orderly tumble of rocks zigzagging like a snake down to the set of large flat rocks perched over the water. Even though the afternoon was beginning to loom, Poppy took the time to inhale deeply, in the hopes that the residue of tree, rocks, and water would linger inside her.

Before heading for the airport, Poppy had planned to make a quick stop to check in on Mrs. Twigg, only a few minutes' detour into West Philadelphia off the Spring Garden Street exit of the expressway. She'd called Mrs. T last night, so she knew she was expected.

Almost a year ago, Mrs. Twigg's dog Red had died, and while Mrs. Twigg was no longer officially a client, Poppy stopped in once every week or two, hoping to convince Mrs.

Twigg she needed a dog. So far Mrs. Twigg was adamant that she couldn't go that route ever again, but Poppy felt that need far outweighed any other consideration, that she was *incomplete* without a dog.

Mrs. Twigg was the only client Poppy had found on her own, in this case as a result of volunteering for the literacy program as a tutor. When they began Mrs. Twigg could only read about the way Poppy could decipher ancient Greek: she knew the alphabet and could sound out the words, look them up in a dictionary, and string them together, painstakingly making sense out of sentences, phrase by phrase. Mrs. Twigg said she thought she had left school after sixth grade, but Poppy suspected she'd left earlier. When they began, Mrs. Twigg had pulled out her worn Bible, but Poppy said firmly, "That's for you to read to yourself. We'll be reading poetry and some fiction and then we'll see." Mrs. Twigg later confessed to Poppy that she'd almost stood up and walked out right then and there, but had been afraid she would never get anyone else, as she had already been waiting for almost a year for a personal tutor.

After two years, Mrs. Twigg was sailing not only through her Bible, but through Zora Neale Hurston and Langston Hughes, Maya Angelou, Toni Morrison, Alice Walker, and many others. She had coaxed her daughter into driving her to a bookstore in New Jersey to get Ms. Angelou's autograph at a book signing! Angelou's was the story of her own life, Mrs. Twigg said, and if that story could make someone famous and respected, then she too had nothing to be ashamed of about her own life.

One day Mrs. Twigg looked Poppy right in the eye, patted her Bible and said challengingly, "This is how the Lord works.

You and me." By now, she knew that Poppy was as skeptical of a benign hereafter as she was of getting real live folks out of the solar system on spaceships, so when Poppy asked, "What do you mean?" she was ready. Mrs. Twigg said, "Hunh, you know perfectly well what I mean, skinny white girl." They stared at each other in silence for a good long while then, Poppy wondering if this was an end or a beginning, until they both started laughing and made so much noise that they were asked to leave the branch library where they always met.

After that Poppy started going to Mrs. Twigg's house in Mantua, right near her old neighborhood. That's how she met Red. At one time his coat must have been a deep glossy chestnut, but with age it had faded to speckled rust. He was clearly of the lineage, special to Philadelphia, of big hammer-headed dogs bred to fight. When Poppy met him he was thirteen or fourteen years old, arthritic, wheezy, and a perfect sweetheart despite having a head that looked like a blunt instrument. No one ever bothered Mrs. Twigg, a tiny woman, when she walked Red. No one ever considered breaking into Mrs. Twigg's house, either.

Well, the long and short was that Mrs. Twigg had developed a very bad bunion and this had to be dealt with, which meant she would barely be able to hobble to the bathroom for several weeks. Poppy, having started the dog walking by then, offered to take Red out. She would have walked him for free, but Mrs. Twigg wouldn't consider that and gave her five dollars a week. Red was too old to need to do much of anything but go around a few blocks at a stately pace, sniffing and peeing on everything.

Horribly, just when Mrs. Twigg had her feet back under her, she woke up one morning to find Red had died in the night.

Even though there was nothing wrong with her, Mrs. Twigg lay back down in her bed and would barely care for herself for a couple of weeks.

When Mrs. Twigg got up she wasn't the same. She wasn't reading her Bible or cooking and with no dog what was the point of walking, so she wasn't exercising either. She sat in her easy chair and watched stupid talk shows.

Before Red died, Poppy had met Mrs. Twigg's daughter Alma a couple of times. Alma had moved back home ten years ago to save money to pay off her loans. She was a nurse at one of the big teaching hospitals downtown and had a crazy schedule. The arrangement worked and she had stayed on even when the loans were paid off.

Alma couldn't have been more different in appearance and affect from her mother. She was tall, broad-shouldered and ebony black, moved slowly and had a grave manner. Her eyes were a startling hazel, very piercing. She and Poppy were cautiously polite, although Poppy was aware that Alma had reservations about her friendship with her mother.

"She takes after her father," Mrs. Twigg said. "He was a big man and dark. All African. No Irish in him," she said. "My father was an indentured Irishman. No white woman would live with him. My mother was lighter than many; her mother had been a house slave." She raised her eyebrows, "That's why I have my freckles and Alma has those eyes of hers."

Catching Poppy looking at the photograph of Alma, proud in her graduation robes, Mrs. Twigg told Poppy how hard her daughter had to work to get her degree as a full nurse, and that even now people, the family members of patients, assumed at first she was an aide because she was so big and quiet.

Alma, who was in the kitchen, shouted, "Say it plain, mama. I look stupid to some people!"

Mrs. Twigg had rolled her eyes at Poppy. "That's how she is!"

Poppy knew she could have made that mistake before meeting Alma.

Besides many photos of the one grandchild, grown and living in New Orleans, there was another photo of a youth in military uniform, finely made with the same lightish skin, freckled nose and cheeks: a dead ringer for Mrs. Twigg. It was Alma who said who he was. "That's my brother, Michael. Our Mikey. He was in the army and he died." From her tone Poppy absorbed she meant that the army had killed him, not combat, and that his had been a wrongful, ugly death. Alma's anger was not at but for him.

Mrs. Twigg, like Irene, disapproved of Poppy's present career, despite its usefulness to her. Since she had benefitted from her tutoring, she thought that Poppy might make a fine teacher. Poppy, aware that anything she said about her present life would sound like a load of horse manure, avoided the topic as best she could. Mrs. Twigg's concern bothered her almost as much as her mother's or Irene's.

Alma agreed with Poppy that her mother should get another dog, and both had been lobbying for Mrs. T to go to the pound to pick one out, a dog from a good home already grown, with good manners and a good disposition. Poppy was even keeping in touch with one of the shelters, but every time they called with a possible candidate, so far Mrs. Twigg had refused to go and meet the dog. Poppy always brought Spock in with her to remind Mrs. Twigg what good company a good dog can be. While Mrs. Twigg always gave him a biscuit and petted him, she defiantly kept her distance.

Red's ashes sat in a little dog-shaped wooden box on the TV set, his photo to one side and a biscuit in a tiny dish on the other, in case he should feel hungry. Once, when Mrs. Twigg left her alone in the parlor, Poppy had whispered to the box, "You can help, you know. Tell her you wouldn't be jealous?"

All this was on her mind today as she rang Mrs. Twigg's doorbell, holding the bag with her lunch in it. She planned to eat her hard-boiled egg and carrot while talking to Mrs. Twigg. She had almost an hour before she had to swing out to the airport to pick up Price, bring him back in to the city, retrieve Clive, and get to the appointment. After that she and Clive would take Price out to their mother's. So far, this all felt doable, if complicated.

Before her finger was off the buzzer, Mrs. Twigg opened the door so fast Poppy knew she'd been standing there waiting. Shouldering her purse and picking up her cane, she shooed Poppy off the stoop, whisked out the door spry as could be, and locked the two deadbolts before Poppy could say anything. She had on her best lavender wool coat and hat and brown zipper ankle boots and Poppy knew immediately this wasn't any ordinary outing.

Turning to Poppy she squared her small shoulders.

"I've picked out my new dog," she said, "Alma and me went yesterday morning. They said twenty-four hours and we could pick her up, but Alma's schedule is all wrong today. They're expecting me. Then we can go to a pet store. She's going to have all her own new collar and leash, bowl and bed, new everything. She's not the same size as Red anyhow. I have my list here." She patted her purse.

Poppy was so stunned she couldn't speak. After a time Mrs. Twigg prodded her gently with her cane. "I thought you wanted me to get a dog."

"I do!" Poppy protested. Truthfully she was struggling to understand why she minded that Mrs. Twigg had chosen to go find a dog at the shelter with Alma, not her. Why had she not said anything last night when they talked? Poppy knew how these kinds of decisions went: for weeks, months, or even years you stubbornly resisted whatever it was and then suddenly, Boom! You're ready to deal, but you have to make it happen RIGHT NOW! as if a little door has opened but you have to step over that threshold quickly because you don't know for how long that door will stay open.

Was there time to pick up the new dog, shop for the items and get Mrs. T and her new dog home before heading to the airport? Maybe, but probably not. All the discount pet shops were outside the city limits. The shopping trip would have to wait.

They had to get the dog. Mrs. Twigg was ready and so was the dog, and the shelter people might not be happy if Mrs. Twigg postponed since this might indicate a lack of commitment. When they got there, Poppy also knew, they would have to act like they had all the time in the world. Any hurry would also make a bad impression.

"Mrs. Twigg," Poppy said, her mind racing, "I do want you to get your new dog. We'll go right now to get her, but I have pick up my brother Price at the airport and then, well, I have to go with Clive to a doctor's appointment. *Then,* I have to take Price out to my mother's house. There is a really good pet store on the way back. So I could either bring you straight home after we pick her up and we can shop later today, or you could stay with us and we'll shop on the way home after I drop off my brother. Or you could give me the list and I will shop for you."

Mrs. Twigg appeared to consider what Poppy had said.

"Staying with you would suit me fine," she said. "I'd like a trip to the country and to see where you grew up. I'd like to do the shopping."

"It's not the country," Poppy said. "It's the suburbs."

Mrs. Twigg did not bother answering.

Poppy immediately regretted offering a choice, she hadn't seriously expected Mrs. T to choose to come along. Both men would be annoyed, and both would have reason on their side. Price would be polite while Clive might be truly flummoxed or even hurt.

She knew how all of them would behave. Price would raise an eyebrow and probably decide to be amused, Mrs. Twigg would be ladylike. From Clive there would be the swift, incredulous glance, followed by a profound courtesy. He always said he *knew* how she was and he *said* he enjoyed the unforeseen complications that sometimes happened around her and so far, maybe he had.

Before pulling out of her parking space, Poppy got out her carrot and boiled egg and took a bite of the egg.

"Aren't you going to ask me?" Mrs. Twigg asked.

"Ask you what?" Poppy said stupidly when she swallowed enough dry egg to talk.

"What *kind* of dog?" said Mrs. Twigg, looking at her as if she had a wig on backwards.

Poppy finished the egg and drank some water, giving herself time to pull her scattered thoughts together. Mrs. Twigg was right: Normally she would be beside herself to know. "So, okay," she said, "what kind of dog?"

"You'll see," Mrs. Twigg said smugly and wiggled herself into the seat more comfortably.

Poppy pulled away and started toward the expressway. "My turn. What changed your mind?"

"The Lord," Mrs. Twigg said. "I was sitting there reading and He spoke to me; he said, 'Vera, you can expect to live a good while yet and you need more company than just Alma coming in and out. Loving one dog doesn't mean you can't love another. Alma says she'll look after any dog I get, should something happen to me, sudden, like happened to poor old Red." She shrugged and looked out the window. "When I got to the shelter I was amazed how different they all are. Just like children. All needing homes."

Poppy's first impulse was to say something lighthearted, but the import of Mrs. Twigg's words penetrated. Mrs. T had been worried about dying; she thought she might be irresponsible to get a dog at her age and that had been what had stopped her. Now she wasn't as worried.

"That's beautiful," Poppy said. "And really nice of Alma."

"You're a good girl," said Mrs. Twigg, still looking out the window as if there were something deeply fascinating in that direction.

Miraculously, Poppy found a parking spot only a block away from the shelter where the car only stuck out a little past the sign. Not in the shade, so she paused to roll down the back windows and to fill a water bowl for Spock. Mrs. Twigg had sped on ahead and Poppy had to hurry to catch up.

As they approached the shelter Poppy was suddenly consumed with curiosity. What kind of dog *had* Mrs. Twigg decided upon? Whatever sort of dog, this afternoon would certainly be a test of its temperament.

She needn't have worried about having to wait. Within minutes of stepping inside, Mrs. Twigg was surrounded by smiling staff people, the center of much attention and approval.

"They are bringing her out," Mrs. Twigg said.

The door from the back regions swung open.

Poppy goggled.

The dog was minuscule, like a Who from a Dr. Seuss book, tiny even for a chihuahua: a tiny, trembly, honey-colored dog. Company, yes, but protection?

Tenderly Mrs. Twigg gathered the little dog into her arms and turned to Poppy, her eyes alight. "How do you like her?" The little dog licked Mrs. Twigg's chin and settled possessively into her cradled arms.

"She's adorable," Poppy said firmly, "do you have a name for her?"

"Indeed I do," said Vera Twigg, going all twinkly, "I'm naming her Poppy Junior after you."

AFTERNOON

A T THE CAR POPPY opened a rear door to let Spock out. From the safety of Mrs. Twigg's embrace, Poppy Junior looked at Spock alert and unfazed, and Spock sat down and wagged his tail slightly. Mrs. Twigg said she'd prefer to ride in back so Poppy leaned in to remove Spock's rumpled towel from the car seat.

She opened the tailgate, shoved around some boxes and bags of books and clothes for Goodwill, and put the towel down for Spock. All the seats were going to be needed for humans.

Mrs. Twigg settled herself as if she was carrying a piece of fragile glass. Poppy lingered a moment with an eye on Spock, not because she was concerned for Poppy Junior's safety but because she could see that Spock was puzzled. The creature in Mrs. Twigg's arms smelled like a dog, but was so small and shivery and delicate, his expression made his thoughts clear that he had doubts whether this was a real dog. He rested his chin on the back of the rear seat where his nose, inches away from Poppy Junior, looked about the same size as her head.

Poppy Junior had no doubts about her status as a dog; she growled imperiously and then barked in a surprisingly robust way at this invasion of her space. Spock's eyes widened and he jerked his head back, his ears going sideways. Then his ears went limp and he curled his upper lip, showing only a little of his molars, while at the same time tipping his head slightly to one side.

He was *flirting*!

"Now will look you look at that," said Mrs. Twigg. "He's gone all goony over her. Just like me."

As she drove toward the expressway entrance, Poppy admitted that having given in to this unwise impulse to take care of everyone, it was more than likely she would fail to take care of any of them as they deserved. She had a feeling that her mind did not hold things in separate compartments the way, by the time you were grown up, you were supposed to be able to do. The day had become entangled with the opposing needs of three people to whom she was committed as either a lover, sibling, or friend, each a relationship that was ordinarily kept separate. Was it enough of a reason that she loved all three?

She had to pay attention to the merge onto the expressway, a difficult one she hated, and her mind moved on. If she could have a moment alone with Price at the terminal, to explain the presence of Mrs. Twigg and Clive's appointment, that would help, but alas, as she pulled up to Arrivals he was already outside waiting. The plane had arrived early, and as he had only a briefcase and very small carry-on bag he had walked right out of the terminal.

In the time she took to walk around the front of the car Poppy noted that Price already looked subtly different. He was more visible. His hair was cut shorter and in a more angular style. His oxford shirt was similar to what he always wore, but tighter and the stripes were lilac on white and his tie was a thin silky thing, silvery grey, perfectly matching a grey buttery suede jacket.

Since middle school days Price had dressed in a style meant for the eye to slide over, neat and unremarkable. Dressed thus, and tall and darkly handsome, he radiated the impression of being a person who was dependable and trustworthy, a person you did not need to scrutinize. Obviously, Poppy understood now, this had been a disguise, a camouflage that had worked splendidly.

Quietly liked and always respected, Price was elected class president or head of whatever organizations he joined; he was the fellow who was smart without being obnoxious, who always spoke carefully and considerately and who could be counted on to keep a secret. While he wasn't much good at sports, he was chosen for teams because he was so good at strategy. A few girls were always interested in him, usually the smart, introspective oddballs, and since middle school he'd had a long procession of opaque relationships with the prettiest of this type. Given that his primary interest, mathematics and computer programming, was known for awkward guys, no one questioned, least of all Poppy, the fact that after a time these relationships always fizzled or faded into friendship.

Stunned as she had been when he came out, her mind, swiftly linking the dots, said: *I should have known!* There was a vague memory from his college years of one of these disappointed women asking her if he might not be gay, a notion Poppy had dismissed and forgotten.

Price was as awkward and unyielding as ever when she hugged him; the carapace of anxiety in which he had enclosed himself was palpable. Was he really that nervous about talking to their mother? Their mother teased a little but was otherwise a remarkably uncritical person, especially about matters close to the heart. Indeed, since one always found fault with one's mother, her children found her to be perhaps too uncritical and too confident that they would all find their way through the world. Her criticisms were rare enough and usually of the bemused, teasing variety. She had remarked that Poppy and Clive had too many pillows and liked calling them the "pillow people." After another of her brothers, Cal (Price's sartorial opposite), turned up in a pair of shoes he had retrieved from a trash bin, she always asked him, "Did you find or buy those?" when he came home in shoes she didn't recognize.

His personal life aside, Poppy was more than a little awed by Price's successes in the adult world. He worked for a private advanced mathematics research outfit associated with but separate financially from Stanford University, meaning they kept most of the money they made and, more importantly, kept copyright of their ideas. Several years ago they had started researching innovative ways to use algorithms to speed up computer processing, and now with the switch from analog to digital and the shrinking of microprocessors and general speeding up and user-friendly advances in computers, possibilities that once required too much processing and were cumbersomely slow had exploded into reality. Price was one of the gurus in this esoteric field of applying algorithms to anything and everything from the hunt for the boson and DNA sequencing to what dog foods sold best. What had begun as purely experimental work without many applications was changing the way information was handled. Price was also making money in ways no one in their family had in several generations.

Of late, when Poppy told people what Price did, there was often a kind of pause when she could see the person thinking, *so what happened to you?* She didn't mind this exactly, that is, having a successful sibling felt good, but equally unnerving was the obvious fact that she was, in ordinary terms, distinctly not on the road to a successful career.

The hug over, Poppy said quickly, "Look, Price. Today has gotten kind of complicated. I have a friend in the car, Mrs. Twigg, because we suddenly had to go get her new dog at the shelter. Then I have to pick up Clive for a follow-up doctor's appointment with this specialist. After that, I will take you out to Mummy's. The thing is I promised to take Mrs. Twigg to a pet store and I can only do that after dropping you off. Anyway, if you don't like this arrangement I can drop you at Suburban Station on the way to pick up Clive."

Price stiffened and his head tipped back, and he eyed her like a startled giraffe. There was a pause. Then he rocked forward and sighed, his gray eyes unreadable. "This has the feeling of one of your plays. I will stick around to see what happens. Lead on."

He picked up his small overnight bag and his briefcase, took them to the back of the station wagon and opened the liftgate. Spock greeted him decorously, his tail waving back and forth in a friendly way. Price patted him on the head, his palm flat; he was as physically awkward with dogs as he was with people but dogs liked him. They recognized trustworthy, dependable, and kind. He stowed his stuff among the boxes and bags, leaving Spock's space clear.

When Price opened the front passenger door, he stuck his head in first and said smoothly, "Hello, Mrs. Twigg, I'm Price, Poppy's brother."

Poppy, arranging her seatbelt, couldn't help but marvel over the fact that all of her brother's awkwardness was physical; socially he was adept—probably because he had learned to protect himself behind an impenetrable shield of good manners.

"It's a pleasure to meet you," Mrs. Twigg replied, very dignified. "Big Poppy has a handsome brother, indeed she does. And this is Poppy Junior," she added, lifting one of Poppy Junior's paws in greeting. "A new member of my family." Poppy Junior blinked, yawned and stuck out a pink tongue that looked exactly like a piece of pickled ginger.

Price's eyebrows went straight up and his eyes touched Poppy's, saying, *Poppy Junior . . . POPPY JUNIOR?* Pressing his mouth in a mirthful line, he closed his eyes to prevent himself from bursting out laughing.

In her George-Washington-crossing-the-Delaware voice of command, Poppy said, "Mrs. Twigg. I am *not* Big Poppy. I am simply Poppy."

"Yes, dear," Mrs. Twigg replied sweetly.

"Or maybe it could be Poppy Major and Poppy Minor," Price said, hunching over.

Poppy drove on, containing her annoyance. Better that he be amused.

"I knew I could count on you," Price said when he recovered.

"For what?"

"To remind me how pointless it is to try to control anything." Price was serious.

Poppy glanced in the mirror at Mrs. Twigg to see if she was listening in. From the look on her face, she was in another universe communing with Poppy Junior.

"Poppy Starkweather, purveyor of random amusement?" she asked, more bite in her tone than she had meant there to be.

"No," Price said in his patient way. "Things have a way of *aligning* around you, perhaps because you let them."

Poppy sniffed. "That's supposed to be a compliment? How has anything I have ever done turned out well? Thrown out of a PhD program for being unscholarly, all I'm good for is walking dogs while you . . . you're unraveling the secrets of the universe."

Price shook his head. "Hardly. You have Clive. You have Spock. You have friends who care about you. My personal life is a wasteland, Pops."

There was a silence. Price turned to look out the window.

Poppy shook her head, "You have a lot of friends. More than I do."

"They are just friends," he said. "I keep everyone at arm's length. You're the closest to me of anyone. You have no idea how often I considered telling you . . ." He stopped and glanced into the back seat, and then said in a lower voice, "But I thought you probably did know. I was always hinting."

"No, I didn't. I had no idea. I didn't get the hints." A relief to say this. She remembered them. Out of the blue he would remark, "I am not a nice person." Or "Oh, you have no idea how wicked I am." And "I think terrible things." She had dismissed these infrequent self-denigrating remarks as part of his perfectionist nature, virtuous to a fault, overly aware of every transgression. She had similar moments. Now she understood he had been warning her that he was deceiving her and everyone else.

Price sat back, unperturbed and perhaps unsurprised. "I know you don't feel great about your professional life, but you'll sort that out. In the meantime, you seem happy to me!!"

In a very small voice Poppy said, "Is it really that bad? Your love life?"

"Pops. All I've done is lie about who I am, so yeah, I'd say it's bad." His bitterness shocked her into silence. Conscious of Mrs. Twigg in the back seat, she said no more. "And as far as the other thing goes, your work life. Your plays," he went on, "the answer might be more obvious than you realize, Pops. Remember UnGrogg?"

They were passing the car crusher near the airport now, a place they had always adored as children. They both looked as a car, windows already smashed out, dangled like helpless prey from the claw that was swinging around to the platform where two huge plates would soon reduce it to the size and shape of a refrigerator. They used to beg their father on his visiting days to drive them there. Happily, some eternal boy in him enjoyed that machine as much as they did, so it was a regular destination.

They both looked at the crusher, Poppy collecting her thoughts. "No, I don't really remember UnGrogg. I made him up, probably, but I had nothing to do with what happened in those plays!" she said with increasing irritation. "You all drove me crazy, you never did a thing I asked . . ." Price stopped her with a small gesture of his hand.

"You don't get it, do you? You don't remember how we were after Daddy left?"

"I remember," said Poppy, "but we all got over it."

"Your plays helped, " Price said.

Poppy shrugged and Price let it drop. It wasn't his way to argue such things. And he was nervous, she could see that. Not the right subject, her problems, to be talking about right now.

Poppy glanced in the rearview mirror; Mrs. Twigg's eyes were closed, her hands gently encircling the tiny dog who lay contentedly in her arms.

"There's nothing to be afraid of, Price," Poppy said tipping her head slightly toward him, "even if that won't stop Mummy from saying something peculiar."

Price's body was compacting as she spoke, until he seemed very small, no more than a boy of eleven, the age, he'd told her, when he knew for sure.

"I know what I *want* her to say," Price said. "Only I can't imagine her saying it and I've never been able to stand disappointing her."

Poppy would have liked to have asked what exactly he wanted their mother to say. She was still wondering if she herself had said what was acceptable (or better), she'd been so flapped she couldn't remember, but apparently she had done all right, or at least Price hadn't noticed how badly she had been fumbling to hide her astonishment.

Despite her sense of having failed him, Poppy's instinct was that Price was depending on her to continue treating him the same way she always had, by taking his affection and tolerance carelessly for granted and vice versa. The good thing was that having him here in person was, so far, anticlimactic. He might look different, but he *was* as he had always been: brilliant, moody, awkward, and the most thoughtful and considerate person she knew. She could only hope that from now on he would tell her the truth about himself and that, for her part, she would pay more attention to what he *wasn't* saying and ask the right questions.

"Has Mom ever been mad or disappointed in you?"

"Hardly ever," Price said. "Except maybe the time I threw up on her lap."

"You couldn't help that," Poppy said, "plus it's one of her favorite stories about you. The whole point being that even your *vomit* has charm."

"It's the only time I can really remember her being mad at me. I wrecked that dress."

"Hunh," Poppy was unsympathetic. "She'd rather die than make you feel she doesn't love you no matter what," Poppy said. "She's that way with all of us, but even more so with you." Everyone knew Price was her favorite; nobody minded because it was Price.

From the intensity of the quiet in the back seat Poppy became aware that Mrs. Twigg had sensed they were talking about serious matters and was listening with ferocious concentration.

"You say that with such conviction," Price said quietly. "How can you know that?"

"I don't, not really, except that I do. Mummy loves you Price, she loves all of us, even me. We're insanely lucky. She's not a judgmental person. Not about us anyway. She's annoying in a million other ways, but that acceptance is real."

"Do you think she keeps her opinions to herself or that she doesn't have any?"

Poppy considered the question. She knew that her mother wasn't thrilled that she seemed to be settling into dog walking as a career rather than as a stopgap, and as well as that she and Clive were taking too long to make up their minds about tying the knot. How she knew her mother held these opinions, Poppy could not say because her mother did not say anything directly about either subject, and anyway, she had only herself to blame for the dog part of it. Conversely, Poppy knew her mother had faith in her ability to sort herself out.

So she said, "A little of both. I mean, she does know us all rather well, so she is entitled to have opinions, don't you think? I'd have to say that she enjoys watching how we work things out. She won't interfere unless it's life or death."

They were off the expressway, merged onto Market Street and crossing over the Schuylkill River, headed for Clive's building.

Hard to say if that answer was what he wanted to hear because Price abruptly changed the subject. "What is this appointment of Clive's about, anyway?" he asked.

"Probably nothing," Poppy said.

As she pulled up to the curb, Poppy could see Clive sitting on a low wall reading the newspaper, one leg crossed over the other. Without looking their way, he snapped the paper closed and stood, having heard, no doubt, the unmistakable growl of the engine. Seeing Clive, Poppy felt a fierce emotion she could hardly contain, as, his newspaper neatly folded under his arm, he moved gracefully toward them. Today though, the feeling was layered with anxiety.

Clive, like Poppy herself, was not an easy person to describe. Essentially nice looking, as Poppy was rather pretty, he shared a tendency to vary in appearance and attractiveness, even if in his case this had more to do with grooming and in hers, state of mind. When immersed in a project, for example, he often ended up looking rather seedy as he liked to wear the same clothes and skip shaving as much as he could get away with. Likewise, at such times he had been known not to notice that a pen in his shirt pocket had leaked or that his shoes were untied. He had abundant hair with multiple crowns and impossible cowlicks that no barber had ever succeeded in taming. His hair only behaved in a buzz cut or long enough to pull back into a pony tail and, being in a line of work creative enough to allow eccentricity, he'd chosen the latter.

Clive's career breakthrough, an odd subset of architecture and design, had occurred when his plans for display cases were chosen for traveling shows of Elvis artifacts. Since then Clive, now a junior partner in the firm, had taken part in assignments as diverse as display cases for a museum within the Arctic Circle in Finland (where the idea was that all materials would resemble ice or snow) to being hired to produce calamity-proof cases for the priceless documents and books that were on public display at the Morgan Library.

"So this is your man?" Mrs. Twigg remarked, sitting up and craning her neck. Poppy, turning to look at her, was struck by how perfectly Poppy Junior fit in her arms.

"Yep," she said.

Price hopped out of the car to greet Clive, who was as easy in his body as Price was awkward. As she watched Price, Poppy supposed some of his awkwardness might not be inherent, but had evolved from the disconnect between who he knew he was and who he pretended to be.

Clive, by contrast, was always present in his body and in that way he was less complicated than either Price or herself. She wasn't clumsy, exactly, but tended to move too fast to pay attention to her surroundings. Clive was also amazingly contented as long as his basic needs were met—food, shelter, company, and something interesting to do (including sex) or think about. That didn't mean he didn't get depressed or anxious or grouchy, especially when overwhelmed with work, but he never questioned his self-worth the way she did. If he couldn't sleep, he got up, made something to eat, and went to work on whatever was bothering him. He'd always sleep fine the next night.

After Clive and Price completed their customary manly yet affectionate greeting—a not-quite hug—Price opened a rear passenger door and hopped in.

Clive got into the front passenger seat. Poppy Junior barked, a sound like a very tiny motor turning over. Clive looked into the back seat, taking in the presence of someone he didn't know.

"This is Mrs. Twigg and . . ." Poppy couldn't bring herself to say the name.

"Poppy Junior," Mrs. Twigg said a little tartly.

Poppy could feel Clive and Price exchange glances.

"Mrs. Twigg," he said warmly. "What a pleasure!" While never having met her before, Clive knew all about Mrs. Twigg and Poppy's desire that she get another dog.

"Poppy Junior," he murmured, and Poppy could feel the suppressed hilarity, "I gather this was an unexpected development?"

"Yes," Poppy said, "I had no idea . . . I was stopping in to check on her and, we had to go, they don't like it at the shelters if . . ."

Clive leaned back in his seat. "It's okay, Pops," he said very quietly, closing his eyes.

Clive's father had died of a heart ailment, a valve defect that is often passed along from one generation to the next. The problem was the shape of some opening, a flap that opens and closes with every heartbeat, which meant imperfect functioning all along and guaranteed early clogging. The problem was rarely life threatening to a young person but became dangerous in middle age (earlier with those who ate poorly and didn't exercise). Clive was fourteen and his father forty-four when he died with no warning. Nowadays, the fix, while not an entirely routine procedure—with the heart there were always risks— had become relatively simple and safe, especially if you could find a cardiologist who specialized.

After Poppy learned from Clive the whys and wherefores of his father's early demise, her first question had been, "Well, do you have it?" He didn't know, and she suggested that was not a good strategy for living a long and happy life and getting to know your grandchildren.

No more had been said about this as Poppy didn't really feel she had the right to insist, but out of the blue a couple of months ago Clive had said, "I've found a cardiologist who sounds good. I've made an appointment to go have those tests."

This was very Cliveish. Most of the time he did not appear to brood, but decided yea or nay on the spot. In some instances, after an inconclusive discussion, months could pass and then out would pop a decision. Poppy had asked him how his process worked and he had answered that he didn't know, except that from time to time he would remind himself that here was a question that needed resolution. "Then one day the answer bubbles up," he said, "or not."

There was a shaded parking spot on the street only a block from the hospital. Poppy knew she would pay and pay for this day's parking karma, but for now she could only be grateful. She showed Price where the stash of quarters for the meters was hidden and handed him the keys, then she and Clive headed down the street to the cardiology department.

Clive had already been here several times for a battery of tests, several of them unpleasant, the last one ten days ago. A heart murmur had been revealed with the first test and this had caused extreme concern, bumping him up the line from exploratory to let's-check-this-out-ASAP. So he'd undergone an EKG, two separate stress tests, an echocardiogram, and finally, using the latest imaging advance, the cardiac MRI (with threats of possibly the worst in store, a cardiac catheter) if the results were still inconclusive. This was a sly defect, not one that openly revealed its existence. A shadow in the x-ray or echocardiogram, plus a sluggish return to baseline after hard exercise, were the clues that would give the cardiologist an accurate picture. These were not doctors who would tell you anything over the telephone, good news or bad you had to come in. At this appointment the cardiac surgeon, having reviewed all the tests so far, would reveal his probable diagnosis, and if he thought it necessary, outline a plan for further information gathering preparatory to surgery.

Poppy and Clive cleared reception and were ushered into a small furnished room where they sat together on a small, slightly spongy, plum-colored sofa. At first they held hands but quickly their palms became too sweaty, so they reduced contact to linked pinkies. Clive had gone completely silent and abstracted.

Poppy looked around. The walls were a calming shade of cool pink, with ivory trim. The artwork, themed on the romantic heart, was tasteful, not kitsch, but an eclectic mix of abstract, whimsical, humorous, and one unexpectedly moving watercolor of a heart evocative of a melting glacier. She wondered how the art had been acquired. Commissioned? Found by the decorator? Or did the cardiologists roam the art galleries on First Fridays, credit cards in hand? Though least likely, the last was the idea she liked best.

A plastic model of a real heart sat unobtrusively behind a lamp on one of the side tables.

When at last the cardiac surgeon, Dr. Croydon, walked in, Poppy felt a wave of relief. From the way his eyes swept over them, she knew that all was well, for in his gaze was a friendly detachment that conveyed: *Thankfully, I will not be getting to know either of you two any better.*

Dr. Croydon pulled a chair up close and sat down, leaning toward them so that Poppy could smell the plain soap and a hint of breath mints. He began talking over the test results slowly and thoroughly, making sure they both understood every step of his thought process and analysis. The essential fact was that Clive's heart murmur was of the "innocent" variety, which meant that when he was active, his heart pumped blood a little faster than it ought to; for the majority of people this feature had no impact whatsoever on their heart health or life expectancy.

Poppy became aware that Clive, who had been so calm throughout, was clutching her hand so hard he was hurting her, and he was breathing in little gasps. Only now was he allowing himself to be terrified. He was okay. The heart murmur was innocent. His valves were perfect. There were many ways to die prematurely, but he would not die the way his father had. This would not be what prevented him from knowing his grandchildren. The doctor was so clear and thorough that neither of them had any questions, unusual for Clive. Poppy's unrestful brain did wonder why use the word "innocent" and wanted to ask what they called the other sort. Bad murmur? Evil murmur? Treacherous murmur? The antonyms all seemed very extreme.

And then they were done. The doctor nodded, smiled benignly, and stood up. They stood up with him. Poppy found her knees were shaky. Gravely they shook hands.

The doctor said, "I love my work, but I like not having to do it even better." He sounded genuine.

When they emerged from the building, Clive stopped, raising his face to the sun as Poppy, feeling lightheaded, stood beside him, hesitating. She did not feel ready to go back to the car. Even though the news was good, they needed time to recover. She knew the hospital had a little garden around the corner maintained for patients and families, so she led him there. He clung to her and she realized he had closed his eyes, trying to squeeze back the tears pouring down his cheeks.

Poppy found a bench and they sat down. Now that the ordeal was over, she understood she had never seriously considered that anything could really be wrong with Clive. She had kept a cool, calm distance from the possibility. Clive had been holding back his fear.

She held Clive's hand firmly and the thought flitted through her mind how rarely that both in a couple cry at the same time, as if you took turns being strong for the other one. Clive turned and hugged her hard, sobbing for another minute, and then he began to rein in.

"I'm thinking about my Dad," he said finally between gasps. "This is so unfair. I get to live . . . even if I *had* the defect, I would get to live."

Then she began to cry, too.

As they calmed down, Poppy became aware that this sunny little garden was so protected that all the early flowers were out, daffodils, hyacinths, and shrubs like the forsythia. Even a few tulips were bravely opening their petals.

Poppy wiped her eyes so she could see them better, thinking that a scientific person could natter on until the end of time about pheromones and stamens and pistils without explaining anything about the human attraction to and identification with flowers. "Flowers," she said, squeezing Clive's hand, "they are so brave."

Clive hiccupped and laughed weakly. "Brazen, even." His face was red and he was sweating, his shirt too was wet, as he sat in a haze, acrid with released tension.

A man in a lab coat entered the garden, stopped and shook a cigarette out of a pack. When he saw them, their swollen eyes and air of sorrow, he frowned and barreled past, exiting through an archway into a further open area, eyes averted.

Clive pulled a handkerchief out of his shirt pocket and mopped his eyes and face and brow, repeating under his breath, "Oh," and "oh, oh," sighing, then repeating the ohs. He looked at the handkerchief, clutched in his hand, and Poppy thought he was going to start weeping again, but he didn't. He stared at the damp square of cloth and sighed and hiccuped. From the handkerchief rose the faint, sharply sweet scent of cherry wood.

One of Clive's unusual quirks was that he always had a clean white handkerchief in a pocket. She knew why he was staring at it. He'd told her the story.

After his dad died, when his mom was as ready as she would ever be, she went through her husband's clothes and possessions. What to keep, what to give away? When she had chosen the items she considered to be special and appropriate she called each of her four children in, one by one, and gave them something to remember him by. For Clive there was a cherry wood bureau topper, with a mirror and two drawers in which his father had always kept about thirty white cotton handkerchiefs, neatly ironed and folded. She had given Clive a leather vest and some cashmere sweaters too, but from then on, even when Clive wore his hair down to his waist, he had always had a clean white hankie folded in a pocket.

Now he smiled at Poppy and spread the handkerchief out flat on his knee, patting and smoothing the soft fabric. As he was doing this Poppy got up and stretched and walked around. When something clanked loudly out in the street, they both jumped and laughed.

Clive said, "Everything looks and feels different, brighter, more textured." He gently folded the handkerchief, stood up, and put it in the back left pocket of his trousers.

They hugged for another long minute. She felt Clive's chest rising and falling as he breathed. She heard his heart firmly beating in his chest.

"So," she asked tentatively, "do you want me to take you back to work?"

"Hell, no," Clive said. "What I would like to do is go home and tear your clothes off."

"Well," she said, not displeased, "that's *not* possible for several hours yet."

"I can wait," Clive said philosophically. "I think I need a little distance from this moment. The threat of death is not a turn-on for me. I'll hang out with you." He took a deep uneven breath.

"And Price and Mrs. Twigg and the dogs," Poppy added.

"With you and your menagerie," he amended.

They stood and kissed and Poppy tucked her arm into Clive's and they left that little paradise.

Price was sitting with his long legs stretched out onto the sidewalk, reading the newspaper Clive had left on the front seat, his burnished leather shoes gleaming. Spock lay on the sidewalk beside Price's beautiful shoes. There was no sign of Mrs. Twigg or Poppy Junior.

When Price saw them, he immediately stood up, folding the paper. Spock sat up too, ears forward.

"Well?"

"Poppy wanted to make sure I'd be around to see my grand-children," Clive said, his voice still rough.

Price's eyebrows shot up. He looked from Clive to Poppy and back to Clive. They were still arm in arm. No doubt it was also obvious they had both been crying hard.

"And?"

"I'm all right. I have a murmur, but it is *innocent.*" The way Clive said it, you could tell he felt very ambivalent about that word in connection with his heart's functioning. "The heart defect my daddy died of, I don't have it." Clive said. Poppy startled, as she always did, at his use of the childish form *Daddy.* The word was so full of love; he had shifted, too, to the more rural cadences of southern Ohio. Neither she nor any of her siblings would ever refer to their father with such natural affection.

"That's great," Price said in a very warm and heartfelt way.

Clive said, "I feel lighter. As if I dropped a heavy backpack I've been lugging around for so long I forgot it was on my back."

They all beamed for a moment.

"Where is Mrs. Twigg?" Poppy said, looking around.

"She's gone off for a little walk," Price said. "I found a piece of twine and we made a tiny collar and she took one of your spare leashes."

"Speaking of which," Clive said, "explain why Mrs. Twigg and, uh, Poppy Junior are with us?"

Poppy explained.

"So now what?" Clive asked. "Do we shop for Poppy Junior or do we take Price out to your mother's house?"

"I offered to take Mrs. Twigg home and come back later to shop, but she said she'd enjoy a ride out to the country. The idea is to stop at a pet store on the way home. I'm sorry Clive, I'm not very good at saying no. I didn't mean . . ."

"Poppy Junior," Clive said savoring the name. He pressed down on Poppy's arm a little and glanced at her fondly, "I know who you are. She named the dog after you."

"A feisty little chihuahua," Price added with delight.

"Don't be jerks," Poppy said, only pretending to be annoyed. "We've got to find Mrs. Twigg and get going. When is Mummy expecting you?"

"I told her you were bringing me out," Price said. "She knows that could be whenever." Both Clive and Price smirked.

Poppy was about to say something snappy when Mrs. Twigg appeared with Poppy Junior in her arms, the two of them cocooned in happiness.

The Vista Cruiser plowed up Spruce Street with a satisfying V-8 rumble. Poppy was thinking about her mother. She wouldn't have any problem with Price being gay, but within half a minute of Price's confiding in her she would do or say something weird; she was the master of the physical and verbal non sequitur. You might be baring your soul and when you stopped to take a breath she would interject, out of the blue, that she had found a giant tick on the dog (she had no dog at present, so at least she would not say that), or that her book group was reading *Coriolanus* and she couldn't think why they were bothering with Shakespeare's worst play, or she'd yank absently on a loose thread and unravel the entire edge of a cushion cover. This made her appear not to care about what you were telling her, but Poppy, who had a little trouble of the same kind, knew that this couldn't be further from the truth; her mother was defending herself from revealing how much she was affected.

As she drove out of the city, Poppy was mulling over her own strategy re Clive. She generally told her mother everything, but she hadn't told her about his heart issue. The main reason was that Clive had seemed to prefer discretion. Her mother was too clever. If Poppy had told her, she would have immediately jumped to the conclusion that having this problem investigated meant they were seriously thinking of marriage.

This trip meant an escalation of her friendship with Mrs. Twigg, she would meet a brother and her boyfriend, would see the house where she had grown up and meet her mother. She was worried that so much information might change Mrs. Twigg's opinion of her.

Mrs. Twigg had worked most of her life for women much like her mother and Poppy had few illusions that her mother was substantially different from any other Main Line or Chestnut Hill matron, and yet the prospect of the two meeting made her nervous. Her mother was a fundamentally good and kind person but Poppy was aware that a lifetime of privilege had made her mother blind to the difficulties most other people face about even the most basic necessities. She herself was probably not all that enlightened either, but at least she did her own vacuuming.

Price broke the silence that had fallen over all of them. "You wouldn't have any aspirin would you, Poppy?"

Clive leaned over and opened up the glove compartment. Out came many items, none of them an aspirin bottle. The glove compartment was quite small, too small for Poppy's needs. One by one he removed several types of lip balm, crushed tissue packs, slips of paper with scribbled directions, old registrations and insurance forms, some pages that had fallen out of her copy of *The Crying of Lot 49*, which Poppy had kept, hoping to tape them back in.

"What have we here?" Clive chuckled happily when he found a pile of recent parking tickets.

"I wasn't hiding them," Poppy said.

Clive was still rummaging about. "I don't think there is any aspirin in here," he said at last.

Mrs. Twigg piped up, "I have some in my bag."

"If you don't mind," Price said. "I get headaches on long flights. The aspirin I took is wearing off."

There was nothing to swallow the pills with except the now cold coffee in the commuter mug, but Price said, "I'll chew and swallow. Thank you so much, Mrs. Twigg."

Clive put everything but the parking tickets back into the glove compartment and began going through them, gloating. Twice a year they tallied up their tickets. She had at least three more parking tickets than he did. Whoever had the most at the end of the year had to take the other one out for dinner.

The quiet now broken, Mrs. Twigg turned to Price and said conversationally, "I would like to fly in an aero-plane before I die. The furthest west I ever got was in a bus to Gettysburg on a school trip with my son Michael, and the furthest north was on the train to Harlem in New York City to visit my sister. The furthest south was by train to my grandma's place in North Carolina."

Aero-plane. Her voice took on a dreamy note as she said the word stretched out like that. "It's very nice that you have come all this long way to visit with your mama. You remind me of my Michael. He was a very good son."

Poppy could have driven the car right off the road or into the back of a bus right then. This was the second time since meeting Price that Mrs. Twigg had mentioned the hitherto unmentioned son.

At last they arrived. Home. This was still home, even though since she and Clive had moved into their own house, she hadn't spent the night here, not even over Christmas Eve.

Poppy turned the wheel and swooped downward into the driveway, not stopping by the garage and kitchen entrance, but steering firmly to the right. Perversely, the front of this house was hidden around the side. She seldom used the front door, but today she would not park anywhere near the kitchen entryway, to be sure of not insulting Mrs. Twigg.

As she passed, Poppy noted that the crocuses around the mailbox (planted with her mother when she was five or six) were already withered. Clumps of the robust early daffodils had begun blooming in the narrow strip of shrubs and trees between the road and the house.

When she turned the car off there was a moment when everyone sat there, listening to the ticking of the engine. On this side, the house had the dour aspect of a Yorkshire manor, all the more so since last autumn when their mother had all the ivy stripped off the stone exterior, which had to be done every ten years, otherwise the stone, a local schist, disintegrated under the fierce grip of the ivy.

The member of the party most pleased to have arrived was Spock, who clattered impatiently on the rubber matting in the back. Concerned that he might trample Mrs. Twigg in his eagerness to exit, Poppy jumped out and went around to the tailgate. Spock bounded out, then froze, nose up and sniffing.

After a few seconds he trotted off to ceremonially pee on the two strangely immobile dogs that held baskets of flowers in their mouths, which sat on either side of the front door and remained puzzlingly unbothered by any insult a living dog might bestow on them.

Everyone else emerged from the car unhurried: Clive, stretching; Price, getting his belongings; and Mrs. Twigg carefully putting the too-heavy leash back on Poppy Junior's makeshift collar.

"I can find you a lighter-weight leash in the house," Poppy said, "and maybe a proper collar," though of this she was doubtful. They'd had a few terriers, but never a dog this small. For several years her mother hadn't had a dog, but all the leashes and collars of previous dogs hung by the back door rather like a canine memorial.

Spock, done with the petrified dogs, vanished through the stone archway heading for the west side of the house. When here, he'd spend most of the time roaming around the four or five undeveloped acres of field that lay to the west and were full to bursting with rabbits. Poppy did not worry; Spock could be trusted not to leave the field or trespass into the suburban development beyond, nor would he venture into the overgrown grounds of the huge estate that bordered the house on the northern side. By the time she was ready to go he was usually to be found either in the kitchen, mooching food off of Sybil, their semiretired housekeeper, or lying in some sunny or shady spot near a door.

Price, heading for the front door, paused. "You coming in with me?"

"No, we'll go look at the garden first." Illustrating intent, Poppy hooked an arm through Clive's. She was in no hurry to see her mother. "We'll be showing Mrs. Twigg around."

She had many reasons to stay outside. She wanted to give Price space. Second, she preferred to avoid her mother until she got over being annoyed about how long Poppy had taken to deliver him. Third, she didn't want to use the front door.

When Poppy was eleven or so, she had developed preferences and aversions about various doors to the outside. The front door was her least favorite, associated with the gloom of *Wuthering Heights*. This door seemed volatile and dangerous, a door of changes, and beginnings and endings, a few good but most not. Newborns came in this way, but this was also the door her father had gone through when he left for good. This was the door out of which she and her siblings had hauled their belongings to go off to college and begin their own lives.

The front door was appropriate for Price today, but she would not use it.

Poppy, passing under the archway into the garden, was aware of slipping into a less coherent self, made up of memory and desire. A more intense and chaotic child self, where impulse and emotion had the upper hand.

Clive, guessing her thoughts, patted Poppy's arm. They had discussed her tendency to blur and become inaccessible when at her childhood home.

The first time he told her this, Poppy was angry and indignant. "You get weird, kind of distant, and then you . . . disappear," he'd said. "Like I don't exist or matter anymore."

After reflection she was able to admit that he was right. Since then she had worked hard at staying present with varying success, relieved that having admitted the effect was apparently enough to have earned Clive's compassion and tolerance.

Clive liked her mother a great deal, which made Poppy happy. They were not unalike, in fact, in some interests and even in some characteristics. Both shared a passion for gardening and neither was much interested in introspection. Clive's idea of a perfect summer day was to come out and grub around in some flowerbed, then make a big sandwich, grab an iced tea or a beer, and head for the shade of the crab apple tree beside the swimming pool, where he happily alternated swimming, eating, chatting, and dozing.

What Poppy couldn't get out of her head was something Irene Childress had said about the first time she had ever spent a night alone in her own house after Mathilde's death. Before that Mathilde had always been with her and during Mathilde's infrequent holidays, Irene had gone to stay with old friends, as if it was unthinkable to remain by herself at home.

When Silas left, last year, her mother faced something similar, although she seemed contented enough.

Poppy then realized that she was hardly any different. She had only rarely had to share a room with anyone until Clive, but she had always lived in houses full of people. The number of nights she had spent completely alone could be counted on one hand. When she brought this up with Clive, he said, "I don't think I've spent too many nights completely alone either, Pops, and most of them have been in horrible hotel rooms. Being alone is *lonely*, Poppy."

Poppy thought of Boswell setting off for London and all the stories of young men going off alone on adventures to find out what they were made of. She hadn't done anything remotely like that. You could, like Boswell, find out you weren't made of what you had hoped you were.

In the myth of Persephone and Demeter, the young woman went from her mother straight to her husband. Nowhere in that myth was there space for Persephone to . . . be. To find out who she was. She only got to be on her own during the brief time *between*, while traveling from Hades to her mother and back again. Was there more to this story than mother and lover vying for the young woman's love and loyalty? Was it disturbing, this assumption, that Persephone, a young woman, had to be with someone, either mother, or husband? Older women, like Demeter, her mother, and Irene, experienced few cultural difficulties around living alone, although perhaps if they were too alone that could lead to ugly clichés about witches.

Mrs. Twigg, led by Poppy Junior, was moving ahead and Clive pulled Poppy gently along in her wake. The day had become very warm and the bright scent of an early blooming mock orange floated on the light breeze.

Poppy Junior, despite being so tiny, moved with authority into this new environment, pausing only to release a microscopic amount of pee beside a concrete rabbit larger than she was. After that, she made for the birdbath, a fancy piece of stone sculpture that had come with the house. There was an upper basin for the birds to bathe in that spilled into a lower one, a moat to protect them from predators while they frolicked. They'd had a cat that used to stalk angrily around and around the rim of the lower basin while the birds, knowing they were safe, splashed and preened above. Maddened, the cat would eventually leap for the upper bowl, but the birds would be gone and he would plunge, soaking wet into the lower basin. That cat was long gone and the fountain was shut off for the winter. Poppy Junior jumped right up onto the rim and down into the empty lower basin, sniffing around as if there were still some trace of the cat.

Poppy glanced into the field looking for the moving dark plume that would be Spock's tail, but saw nothing.

Clive and Poppy went along, following Mrs. Twigg and Poppy Junior, passing the gloomy porch off her father's study, where he used to sit smoking and where, as adolescents, she and her siblings would go to smoke pot. (The porch door off the study was *Narnia* because once they stepped through, they seemed to become invisible to all adults.) They ambled past the French doors of the living room next. *Pride and Prejudice*, those doors were opened mainly for parties and holidays.

She glanced into the big room, which appeared to be empty. Price and her mother would still be in the kitchen, making up a tray of tea things and cookies. They would come here to the living room where they would sit in the armchairs by the fireplace and chat inconsequentially. (Price was renowned for not bringing up what he really wanted to talk about until at least half an hour into a phone conversation or visit.)

Mrs. Twigg stopped suddenly and said, "So, Miss Poppy, this is where you grew up." Her eyes seemed very big, her freckles more prominent.

Poppy winced and nodded. She hated when Mrs. Twigg called her Miss Poppy.

At this moment Poppy Junior spied another concrete figure—of a very large snail—and started to bark with so much vigor that she bounced, all four paws about a foot off the ground.

They all laughed, then Mrs. Twigg picked up her dog and walked on.

Clive had fallen behind and was standing at the top of the half-circle stairs that led down to the perennial garden where a few green clumps were starting to put up new shoots that would later become iris, peonies, daisies, poppies, and more.

Poppy wondered what he was thinking about, nothing too convoluted or fanciful; Clive's mind tended toward planning what he was going to do next. He was probably thinking about his plans for his own garden or musing over ideas for a future garden if they ever had their own house "in the country."

There couldn't be much left to do at home, for Clive had taken their tiny in-town garden about as far anyone could. When they'd moved in, the backyard, about ten by twelve feet, had been paved over and bare of all but a pair of fake barrels filled with marigolds (probably purchased and planted by the real estate agent). The first summer Clive rented a jackhammer and tore up the pavement, laid brick and stuccoed the walls in a soft coral shade mixed up from watercolor samples he'd made on a trip to Tuscany in college. Last summer he'd made the little deck and arbor and planted grapes and found a tiny table and chairs that fit. He had mentioned espaliering fruit trees onto the walls next so maybe he was thinking about that.

She looked again and saw that Clive was not looking at the garden, but to the side at the rusted swing set and the weedy remains of a sandbox where, as a child, she'd gotten impetigo. Near the sandbox was the small crab apple that had been everyone's first climbing tree. She couldn't help but admire the easy way Clive stood there conveying readiness and confidence in his ability to take on anything from gardening to being a parent. She thought of the youthful Peer Gynt, how fanciful and peculiar that play was: yet here stood a young man who looked as if he could leap over mountains. It made Poppy's heart hurt.

With the question of his health settled, he would ask. He might have a little satin or velvet box tucked into a pocket. He might be wondering how he would know it was the right time and place to propose.

Not here, Poppy thought. *Not now.*

They hadn't exactly rehearsed but they had nibbled around the edges of the question and Poppy had never given Clive any reason to think she might say no. From his point of view, Poppy knew, the heart test settled everything. He'd even once inquired if she would like him to formally ask her father for her hand, but dropped the idea when Poppy snorted contemptuously.

She can feel the future pressing up, insistently from Clive—yes, in a very male way, pressuring her. Why did she mind? He was, yes, a catch! He loved her! She loved him! He would not, she thought, tolerate the idea of "just living together," interpreting that to mean she was not committed. She was being perverse and not even honest with herself. If she did want to be with anyone forever it was Clive, but she didn't want to be anyone's *wife*. How she loathed the word "wife"! But what choice did she have? Imperfect as marriage was, this was what humans did, this was the foundation of adult life. This was how adults staved off loneliness. Poppy made an involuntary groaning sound and Clive turned around, smiling so happily she almost groaned again.

Until meeting Clive she'd never once thought of herself marrying anyone or of being someone's wife and calling someone else, "my husband." (She didn't think it possible that that phrase would ever roll easily off her lips.)

Clive felt differently. She had a feeling if she asked him he would admit, without embarrassment, that he had always figured he would marry, and she suspected that girls would have targeted him to play the groom in those kindergarten games. She'd never been interested and no one had ever asked her to participate; she was far too busy pretending to be a horse. The closest she had ever gotten, as a child, to domestic role playing was when she and Price had gotten into building dream houses in the playroom. They had built their own places, and she could not remember ever mentioning partners or family, although she might have had a stuffed dog that she "walked." They were just two people, neighbors and friends, living alone.

"We'd better catch up with Mrs. T," Poppy said, taking Clive's hand, feeling the work calluses, "she'll like the rose garden even with nothing blooming yet."

The roses, in their protected corner, were doing nothing. Most were still bagged in burlap, but her mother had taken off a few coverings and those stalks had knobs of vivid green. Poppy's mother hadn't started out liking roses or even gardening particularly, but she had inherited this rose garden from the previous owner who had left behind her personal gardening journals and an old hat.

When her mother read the journals she learned that these were not ordinary roses, but painstakingly collected Old European varieties, Damasks and so on. There was a Bermuda mystery rose, so rare that her mother worried about its safety enough to give it an incorrect label. Only a couple of her closest friends knew the truth. Clive knew because he'd asked her mother directly when he couldn't find a mention of this rose's color and appearance (under the false name) in any of his reference books. The rare rose was on the small side, the palest parchment yellow, with dark rose edging and minute streaks of lavender down the petals. The smell was very sweet and suggestive of apple blossoms.

Poppy veered away from the rose bed to the swing that hung from a high limb of the gigantic and still healthy elm. She sat on the seat, feeling the thick ropes bounce. Idly, she swung. The ground was still packed so hard that nothing ever grew, even though the swing was never used anymore. She could recall how once she'd had to stretch her toes to touch the ground and now she had to bend her ankles awkwardly to keep her feet from scraping.

Then she couldn't wait to be grown up, and now she would give almost anything to go back for one more of those magical nights, fireflies sparking in the meadow, her father in a jovial mood, setting up a telescope outside the living room door to be pointed at the moon or Mars or Saturn's rings, whatever he had decided he wanted them to see. The three older ones, the girls, were allowed to stay up for this special treat, running wild while waiting for proper dark.

Clive came over. Mrs. Twigg had wandered to the Pan fountain (when operational, water jetted out of the pipes in Pan's mouth) and was sitting on the rim, Poppy Junior in her lap.

"I'm starved," Clive said, "I was too nervous to eat lunch and I'm guessing Mrs. Twigg might be hungry too and thirsty."

Immediately remorseful, Poppy jumped up. They collected Mrs. Twigg. As they crossed the lawn, Poppy glanced toward the big field and this time spotted the black tip of Spock's tail.

They went in through her favorite doors, French, glass paned, facing south, that let abundant light into the main hall. Through this door they had all, as children, galloped out in a whooping mob clad in bathing suits or snow suits or pyjamas to swim, build snowmen, or have one last pre-bedtime ride on the swing. You could go out this door when your homework or chores were done and when school was out. In good weather, their parents often sat on the flagstone terrace outside this door, shaded by the elm. Often there had been a baby carriage set near, netted, with a sleeping infant inside. Moley from *The Wind in the Willows* stirred by her friend Ratty to adventure, would have come out this door.

As Poppy stepped into the hall, she was assailed by smells—the epitome of home, as defined and achieved by her mother. This, her nose said, is how a *real* home looks, feels, and smells. Orderliness. Meals on time. Folded, sweet-smelling laundry. Flower arrangements. Polished wood. Amplitude. You couldn't tell, entering this house, what anyone ate for dinner last night or whether there was a cat.

At her, no, at *their* house, you encountered the fish from last week, the foot odor from shoes lined up in the hall, the piquant funk of dog on the sofa. From upstairs floated the tang of mildewed shower curtain and from the basement, even with a dehumidifier always running, an odor at once sour and damp escaped every time she went up or down to do laundry. If you opened the refrigerator a concerto of celery and stale onion, of old cat food and lunchmeat past its due date might invade as far as the living room.

Of course, larger houses don't collect and retain odors the way smaller ones do, and her mother had always hired people for the heavy cleaning, dusting, and polishing. Yet even without support her mother effortlessly created a certain ambience. Poppy had shared hotel rooms with her upon occasion and even when her mother had only a small suitcase and no special props, her belongings behaved. Her bed always looked neat and inviting. By the bed, her clock worked; there was a small dish for her rings, a book, a small flashlight, all neatly arranged. Her shoes lined themselves up. She always had everything she needed, and an extra of whatever it was you had forgotten, like your toothbrush or band aids. Come to think of it, Clive was that way too.

As Poppy stepped inside a few more layers of her adult self peeled away. *Poof!* She paused, listening. Yes, her mother and

Price were in the living room now; the murmuring of their voices flowed out of the tall doors. They would be sitting in the big green-and-white armchairs on either side of the fireplace, the tea tray on the low table between them and Price's favorite cookies, Lorna Doones, spilled onto a plate.

Suddenly famished, she hurried after Clive and Mrs. Twigg.

EVENING

DESPITE LIVING ALONE most of the time now, their mother continued to food shop as if half of her children were living at home. Favorite foods were always in plentiful supply. For Mel there were salty wheat biscuits; for Clemmy, sandwich cremes; for Cal butter pecan ice cream; for Price the Lorna Doones and home-baked cinnamon raisin bread, sliced, in the freezer; for Silas there were macadamia nuts; for Poppy there was always swiss cheese and tomato to make a grilled sandwich. The foods were never moldy or stale. How their mother managed this feat was a matter of speculation; the favorite theory was a supernatural relationship with the A&P.

Poppy and Clive swiftly assembled a platter of ham, baloney, lettuce and tomato, sliced swiss and cheddar cheeses. Inelegantly, she propped a knife in the jar of mayonnaise; her mother would have spooned some into a shallow dish. Clive put out a box of cookies. From the bread bin Poppy pulled out a homemade loaf. Poppy and her sisters had been mad bread bakers in their teens and while they had quit long ago, their mother had continued. Poppy sliced off several pieces, putting a couple in the toaster. The teakettle started to whistle.

"This is very delicious," Mrs. Twigg said, sipping her Earl Grey and nibbling a cookie with chocolate filling. She offered a small piece of cheese to Poppy Junior in her lap, who daintily accepted it. Clive made two sandwiches and ate them one after the other, and then ate a few cookies.

At last, as she knew he would, Clive gave Poppy a querying look, eyebrows slightly raised and not hard to read: *When can we go home?*

Even though she knew she was being unfair, Poppy felt instantly irritated by this and made a tiny shrug. *I don't know.* He would be attributing her reluctance to leave to the state she got into here, indecisive and uncommunicative. Yes, but he knew she would not leave without saying hello to her mother and checking in with Price.

Mrs. Twigg suddenly arose, put Poppy Junior down, and made off in the direction of the bathroom, which had been pointed out when they first came into the kitchen in case she needed to "wash her hands." The little dog followed her, tiny nails scratching on the linoleum. The two had instantly become attached, Poppy observed, so despite Poppy Junior's uselessness as a guard dog, she would be good company. Perhaps that mattered more.

After Mrs. Twigg closed the bathroom door, Clive took another sip of tea and then asked, attempting cool neutrality, "What are we waiting around for?"

"Until Price finishes talking to Mummy. And you know perfectly well I can't leave without saying hello to her."

"How long do you think it'll take him to tell her?" Impatience was creeping into his tone.

"Clive." Poppy stared. "You agreed to this. You knew how it would be. It's Price. Who knows?"

"Pops," he said, tapping his fingers on the table, "I'd like to go home."

He raised his eyes and looked at Poppy directly. His eyes, ordinarily a cloudy sort of blue, had a frosty edge. He was fed up and, she thought, probably wanted, above all, to go home to have sex. Was counting on it. Not unreasonably, Poppy thought.

"I'll finish my tea? Then I'll go in and say good-bye."

"I'm not letting you in there," Clive said grumpily. "Your mother won't let you go, especially if she thinks you are in any kind of hurry. Really, we could just go. Under the circumstances."

Poppy stared. "She doesn't know the circumstances, Clive. And she doesn't know we have Mrs. Twigg here unless Price told her, which I doubt."

Clive shifted uncomfortably and seemed to relent.

Poppy frowned. She did want to check in with Price, but she was relieved Clive did not seem to want to tell her mother about the heart tests, so maybe it would be best to leave and deal with the consequences.

Clive gave in. "Alright, I'll say hello to her and that we have to go. Let's hope Price has gotten around to telling her." Clive left and Poppy didn't stop him, although she was in no hurry to leave. She never was once she was here. *Let's see how he does disentangling from Mummy!* she thought. *He thinks it's so easy!*

Less than a minute after Clive departed, Mrs. Twigg returned to the table. Poppy Junior pottered along on her ridiculously thin legs and sniffed the undersides of cabinets. Mrs. Twigg looked into the teapot, then poured the remaining tea into her cup, and said casually, "Your boyfriend seemed real happy when you came back from that appointment."

"His father died young of a heart defect," Poppy said. "They can fix that problem now, so he went to find out if he has it. He doesn't."

Mrs. Twigg nodded. "He looks at you like he wants to eat you up!" She laughed as Poppy blushed.

"Sweetheart," Mrs. Twigg said then, "I won't deny you are my favorite white person ever, but I'd like to go home very soon. I want to show off my little girl to my neighbors." She finished off with coy suggestiveness: "And you need to get home too."

"I know," Poppy said. "Clive is telling Price and my mother that we have to go." She stood up and began to clear the table, putting food away and rinsing dishes and cups to put in the dishwasher.

She was about to turn on the faucet when she heard a male cardinal in the rhododendrons outside the window making its special territorial clicking sound. Less than a foot from the window, the bright red bird swayed on a branch.

"Oh, come look!" she exclaimed to Mrs. Twigg, who rose and came over. They stood by the sink, rapt. The cardinal was so close they could see the shine of his beak and black eyes, his head in perpetual motion, turning and dipping, his feathers and crest rippling in a stray breeze. When he lifted off they believed they could hear the silky rustle of his wings.

"That was nice," Mrs. Twigg said contentedly, "I do miss the country sometimes."

Poppy's attention returned to the dishes. Clive had not returned, no doubt caught in her mother's comfortable net. When she finished washing up she would call Spock in.

Mrs. Twigg exclaimed in alarm, "Now where's my Poppy Junior gone off to?"

They both looked around. Tiny as she was, she was obviously not in the kitchen anymore.

"She must have taken off while we were looking at the cardinal," Poppy said, thinking maybe that was how she ended up at the shelter. Some dogs are like that, independent and curious, seizing a moment of inattention to explore. "No worries, Mrs. T," she added firmly, "she's inside somewhere. All doors to the outside are closed. I'll find her."

Poppy jogged down the corridor to the front hall to check that she had properly closed the door to the outside. She had. In the living room she could hear Clive's voice mixed in with her mother's and Price's; it wasn't, as she knew it wouldn't be, the tone of a voice on the verge of departure. He was laughing. They were having an animated discussion and her mother was being warm, funny, and irresistible. Poppy Junior wasn't in there or they would have been talking about her, and anyway Clive would have brought her right back to Mrs. Twigg.

Mrs. Twigg had followed Poppy and was waiting on the landing, frowning, "I can't call her, she don't yet know her new name and we don't know her old one."

"She hasn't run away," Poppy said. "She's exploring. Maybe she thinks this is her new home." She pointed to the dining room. "You check in there; I'm going to check out the library. We'll meet back in the kitchen."

The library was the other room their mother had done over, but even painting the bookshelves white and putting cheerful yellow chintz on the armchairs and sofa couldn't do anything to change the fact that the room had inadequate light, as the only window was shadowed by the porch.

When Poppy returned to the kitchen, Mrs. Twigg was looking very upset. "Maybe a bigger dog would have been better. Junior could fall through a itty-bitty hole and be gone forever."

"There are no itty-bitty holes anywhere in this house," Poppy said, "and all the doors to the outside are firmly shut." She repeated, reassuring herself as much as Mrs. Twigg, "She can't get outside."

She kept to herself the hamster that had escaped and died in a bucket in the basement, but checked that the basement door was shut. "She has to be upstairs exploring. I'll run up there and take a quick look around. Don't worry. We'll find her."

On her way up, Poppy called, "Junior? Hey, little girl, where are you?" knowing she was wasting her breath.

After checking the rooms and bathroom that served the three small bedrooms in the former servant's wing, Poppy pushed through the door into the main house.

For her last years at home Poppy had moved into one of the back rooms over the kitchen. Since then she rarely entered the upstairs of this side of the house. When she did, she always thought of her father.

Despite his lack of interest in children, their father's destiny was to be inundated: eight so far, the six of them and two more in his second marriage. When he left and when they divorced, he had asked for nothing but to be released from all financial responsibilities. In return, he would make no demands. As their mother had plenty of money and he had very little, she agreed as long as he regularly saw his children.

Her brothers Silas and Cal were the sunniest children in the family. They didn't remember what it was like when Daddy still lived with them. The main thing was how confusing it was, the okay and even fun times such as during the telescope craze alternating with times when he seemed to view them as obstacles set in his path. He had a beastly temper and when angry he yelled and cursed and even though the anger came and went quickly and he never threw objects at or hit anyone, it was frightening to small children. He rarely touched or kissed any of them; an occasional hug or a pat was about all he could manage.

Even when he was physically present, he was absent, often talking to himself, as if unable to move outside the bright, shifting landscape of his inner life. While he was not incapable of kindness, he appeared to forget, for long stretches, to exercise affection. All too often the only reason he became aware of his children was because they had interrupted his thoughts and irritated him.

Sometimes, unexpectedly, he would suddenly notice you, which could be good or bad. For instance, Poppy always stirred her ice cream into a soup she could eat without her teeth hurting. One night when she might have been seven or eight he put his spoon down and inquired sarcastically what she was doing. "Making ice cream soup," she said. "It's not soup," he said, "it's ice cream. You're supposed to eat it cold. If you don't stop, I'm going to take it away."

Poppy had started to cry. "But I have to, Daddy! The cold makes my teeth hurt! I'm trying to hurry the melting. You've seen me do this a million times!"

Her father had stared at her, then threw his napkin on the table and left muttering. When Poppy looked at her mother for sympathy, she had sighed and said, "Just finish up, Pops, we're all waiting for you."

Another time, her father, coming home, found Poppy watching Mel and Clemmy riding their bikes and doing fancy stunts in the driveway, and asked, "Why aren't you out there?" She told him she didn't know how and didn't have a bike, anyway.

"You don't have a bike?" He was scandalized.

They'd gone right to a bike shop to buy a bike and a set of training wheels, which he had put on with surprising dexterity; then they worked until dinnertime. Every couple of days he raised the wheels higher and then ran around and around the driveway with her. Ten days later, he took the training wheels off and vanished into his study. All the older ones had had experiences like that. You couldn't hate him.

Poppy listened, while letting the waves of memory pass through. Straight ahead down the long corridor was her mother's room over the living room and she started to go that way, but suddenly veered to the left, into the short hallway to the stairs to the third floor. She'd start there, work down.

There was no way Poppy Junior would be on the third floor, but Poppy had a sudden intense desire to see the old playroom. The last time she'd been here was when showing the whole house to Clive the first time she'd brought him out. She'd be quick. Anyway, where she looked first hardly mattered: the little dog couldn't be in any real danger.

As she went up, Poppy was aware of the ramp above her head, hung on thick ropes that, by gently pulling down a lever, could be lowered to shut off the third floor from the rest of the house. The mechanism was so perfectly balanced that a ten-year-old could easily raise or lower the ramp, but that was strictly forbidden. Silas and Caleb, as teenagers, believed the ramp prevented the smell of pot from leaking down and ignored the rule. (For the record, it didn't.)

She passed by the bedroom that Silas and Caleb had taken over when Price left for college. On one epic occasion when Silas was in eleventh grade a girlfriend had stayed for an entire weekend, no one the wiser.

The playroom, when Poppy arrived at the door, looked as it had after their mother had sent them to clean up. The huge room, spanning almost the whole length of the house, retained, more than any other room except maybe the butler's pantry, the air of a distant era, 1906 when houses like this one had nurseries, school rooms, servants' quarters, flower-arranging rooms, and a butler's pantry.

The floor was cork tile to absorb the sound of running feet. On the walls, unevenly pasted, were yellowed photographs from ancient *National Geographics*. At the near end a huge glass-fronted bookcase was so jammed full of books, they pressed on the panes. Most were her family's books but many had been left behind by the previous family—ancient atlases with maps of the world replete with names long left behind, Barbary, the Belgian Congo, Tartary, the Russian Empire, Nippon, Hindustan, and British Canada, and novels about sappy girls and brave boys. (Poppy was the only one who had even attempted to read them.) The lower cabinets were bursting with games, puzzles, dolls, and the remains of chemistry and erector sets.

Along one side of the room a false house front had been whimsically fitted into a large dormer; a child-size door was flanked by functional sash windows. Painted on was a picket fence, teeming with morning glory vines. Inside, there was only an enormous cupboard where, as Silas put it, "toys came to die." Daddy's much-missed ivory-handled razor, passed from father to son for several generations, turned up, the ivory cracked, as did a broken silver candlestick, a bent bicycle wheel mysteriously not belonging to any of their bicycles, and once a skull that Silas had stolen from the school science room as a prank.

Her mother hadn't touched a thing. The gigantic yellow sofa sat huge and predatory, the ping-pong table beckoned, and the limp curtains and drooping costumes of the rehearsal space at the far end of the room seemed to be waiting for their return.

Obviously Poppy Junior was not here, but Poppy lingered in the quiet, relieved to be alone.

The last significant time she had spent here was with Price after their father left. Their two older sisters were entering adolescence, the two younger brothers were too little to be any fun, and Poppy and Price were suddenly thrown together.

The game began one day when they ascended to the play-room (probably out of desperate boredom) and came up with the idea of building "dream houses." They started with the sofa cushions and big cardboard bricks and soon began sneaking downstairs to pilfer blankets, sheets, bathmats and anything else they could safely snitch to make walls, beds and rugs.

From the start an unusual spirit of cooperation prevailed, unusual because Poppy and Price had not previously gotten along well. The yellow sofa had six "good" cushions, and they scrupulously shared three apiece. If you went treasure hunting, you would return with one thing for yourself and something you thought the other might find useful. They never discussed these protocols; it just seemed obvious to them what would work best. They would labor in silence except for necessary discussion about construction problems and consultations on aesthetics. As no one else ever came up to the playroom anymore, their "houses" could evolve for months.

Outside all you would see was a messy checkerboard of sheets. No matter, all they cared about were the interiors. For "pictures" they would liberate scarves from their mother's vanity, hanging them up on the "walls" with safety pins. They crafted ingenious beds, desks, and tables out of camping gear and lumber stored in the basement. Extension cords were found. (When the lamps were discovered there was trouble.) After that they'd had to rig inferior setups using flashlights.

Once the building phase was over, they inhabited their houses. Price made a "desk" and spent hours drawing. Poppy lay on her bed, read books and copied sentences she liked, wrote a poem or two, and ideas for her plays. In a few hours they would live several "days,"—getting up and going to work, shopping, coming home. After a period of quiet one of them might call out, "Time for tea?" Discussion would ensue about whose turn it was to host, what they would eat, which would be followed by feverish preparations. When all was ready, the host would open the towel door with a ceremonial flourish and the guest would enter.

They would eat and drink, imitating the formal visits they made on Sundays to see their great aunts.

In the present, remembering, Poppy's mind halted.

What on earth had they talked about? They were eight and ten! They could hardly have talked about what was really in their minds, such as, "How do you feel about Daddy leaving us?" or "Did you notice that Mummy was crying earlier?" or "I got punished for daydreaming in school again today."

Had they made small talk? If so that was ironic, as neither of them was good at the art as adults. Probably they hadn't talked much beyond "pass the cookies" or "more tea, please." The tea parties represented civilized behavior. As with building the houses, setting a fine table, finding and sharing food and candy, and pretending cold water was tea, planning and preparing was far more interesting than the event.

During the year or two of playing this game, Poppy and Price had developed their friendship, built on solving problems, sharing food and treasures equitably, proving trustworthy, and having secrets of their own apart from the others.

As Poppy moved into the room she could see that someone had been up here. A deck of cards lay on the ping-pong table, a teacup and saucer sat on the low table beside the huge yellow sofa, and on the arm a book of Walter de la Mare's poetry had been left open, face down.

Peering into the cup, she saw a brown stain and stray tea leaves, strewn about like dead ants. Her mother drank this particular kind of tea, strong and smoky, in the late afternoons and she was the only one who used these teacups. Limoges, hand painted with tiny colorful birds.

Poppy abruptly sat on the slippery silken brocade of the huge sofa.

Their mother would only come up here if she were missing them. She never did admit to it directly, instead saying things like, "Now that I don't have all you tumbling about spilling and breaking everything, I can do as I please."

Then why had she done nothing to this room?

Poppy picked up the book on the sofa arm. Ah. "The Listeners."

"'Is anybody there?' said the Traveller." She remembered a teacher asking them to comment on the use of "said" not "asked." Someone wondering if it was about ghosts? The past. "Never the least stir made the listeners, / Though every word he spake / Fell echoing through the shadowiness of the still house / From the one man left awake . . ."

Poppy put the book down, appalled to think of her mother sitting up here by herself. She had surrounded herself with children, but you couldn't prevent them from growing up and leaving eventually.

Poppy's mother had been orphaned by fifteen. Her parents married late and died somewhat young—first her father when she was ten, and then her mother. Her two older brothers, in college and the army, came home briefly, but soon her mother was left alone.

"After my mother died," her mother had said, "everyone was trying to decide where I should live. They couldn't decide which household would be the best for me. Should I live with my Aunt Bet and Uncle Ned who had six children, all older than me, or with Aunt Meliora, a spinster who had been closest to my father?" The family, with strong Quaker roots, debated the matter for several weeks until they agreed that Anne would go live with Aunt Meliora. The "big house" would be closed. Aunt Meliora told Anne to choose any furniture she liked to have moved into her new room.

"That last day, after my belongings and the furnishings I'd chosen were all taken away," her mother once told Poppy, "I sat on the porch stairs all afternoon looking out over the field down to the river. For some reason I became quite sure that if I didn't budge, my mother would drive up, laughing and talking in her jolly way. If I left those steps, I knew there was no chance she would ever come back.

"Aunt Meliora walked over and tried to coax me to come with her, but I wouldn't move. Aunt Bet and Uncle Ned came and sat on either side of me and hugged me. In the end, the farm manager and his wife, Mr. and Mrs. Jack, drove up in the big red farm truck and Mr. Jack, who could carry a grown sheep, picked me up like I was a little lamb, which I wasn't, and carried me to the truck and put me in between them. They took me to their house for tea and scones and then they walked on either side of me down to Aunt Meliora's."

A year later, Daddy was the first man her mother fell in love with: tall, handsome, witty and charming, the best friend of the younger of her two brothers from boarding school, the two were now roommates at Harvard. Anne was too young for lifelong declarations but she made them anyway; Aunt Meliora took her on a long trip out West, but nothing stopped her. Even if Daddy had doubts she would have swept them away. They married after her first year at Wellesley and she swore to the authorities she would not get pregnant. Mel was born ten months after the wedding. After that, a child came every couple of years. Her mother loved babies, liked little children, tolerated older children and adolescents with good humor, and was a good friend to those of her grown-up children who were ready for that paradigm.

Poppy stared at the scattered tea leaves. When she looked at his predicament from her father's point of view, she couldn't really blame him for leaving. To wake up one day, at thirty-one (only five years older than she was now), to discover yourself surrounded and outnumbered by little beings who are even more self-absorbed than you, who never shut up, and never leave you alone to think.

When she played the house game with Price they had lived alone; there was no chatter about families and friends and social lives, nothing much about careers either. They called what they did when they built their houses, when they read and wrote and were drawing, and when they prepared for a tea party "work," but it wasn't job or career work.

These days when someone asked Poppy what she did, she said, "I walk dogs and drive around." The person's head would tilt, "Really?" Whereupon she would say, "Seriously. That's what I'm doing." She could see them trying to think of a tactful next question and failing, moving to another topic.

When his father called an end to the London experiment, Boswell had gone home to make a start at doing as his father had wished, studying law and later marrying and settling down. He had kept writing his journals and his books about the men he admired, an interesting group, radicals and original thinkers all—Johnson, Paoli, and Voltaire—and his writings did earn him some of the celebrity and respect he craved. Once a year he went to London and was happy.

She let her head flop back against the sofa.

Poppy heard her name being called, not Poppy Junior, but Poppy.

She'd completely forgotten she was supposed to be looking for Poppy Junior!

Someone was clumping down the hall. Abruptly she stood up, still holding the teacup on its saucer.

"Poppy, what are you doing all the way up here?" Clive appeared.

"Looking for Poppy Junior," Poppy said, unconvincingly.

"We found her in your mother's room," Clive said, impatiently, "she's eaten a bag of chocolate-covered cherries that were stashed in the cushions of a chaise longue. We're wondering if we have to call the vet."

"Damn," Poppy said. "How many?"

"Your mother thinks there were only a few candies left," Clive added. "So probably she's okay." He looked at her for confirmation. "Your namesake really is a very small dog."

"Oh, I see, I'm the expert. Let's go see," she said, putting the teacup and saucer down on the ping-pong table.

"You were drinking tea up here?"

"No," Poppy said, "Mummy must have come up sometime."

Clive grinned, looking around. "I'd forgotten about this wonderful room," he said. "It must have been so much fun to play in. Your mother has told me about your plays, how odd and unexpected they were."

Poppy uncrossed her arms and eased into a less defensive posture.

"They were daft, those plays," she said dismissively. "All I did was set people in motion. Everyone did whatever they felt like. No one did *anything* the way I wanted."

"That's not what your mother says. She says that in each play something wonderful always happened."

Poppy shrugged, as if to say, *what do you expect? She's my mother.*

"You sneaked up here to get away, didn't you?" Clive said, changing the subject.

"I did not sneak," Poppy said and then stopped and shrugged. Why deny what was true?

The six or seven feet between them encouraged truthfulness.

"All right, yes, I sneaked off," she admitted. "For your sake, I am sorry about today."

Clive stood a little straighter as if anchoring himself. "That's good to know," he said. "I was beginning to wonder if . . ."

"I'm not an idiot, I know the point of the . . . the test," Poppy said, interrupting him, her voice croaky. "I'm afraid I . . ."

Spock clattered unexpectedly into the playroom dancing up to them, but catching the tension paused, his ears moving back and forth, picking up signals.

Price called, sounding more peeved than frantic.

"I guess we'd better go," Poppy said.

"Wait," Clive said taking her hand as she moved past him. "What were you saying? What are you afraid of? Me?"

"No. Not you." Poppy didn't pull away. His hand was warm, hers cold. "Me. I can't talk about it now."

Clive looked bewildered. He let her hand go. She was disappointing him, by being difficult and selfish. She was possibly behaving like some character in a book who does or says the one thing that creates a misunderstanding, a delay, a maddening mix-up, or worse, sometimes total disaster.

She couldn't let him propose. Right now, in the state she was in, she would choke on Yes.

They found Price, her mother, and Mrs. Twigg standing in a circle in the hallway. As one they all turned to look at Poppy, Clive, and Spock. Then they all returned to anxiously studying Poppy Junior, who lay subdued and inert in Mrs. Twigg's arms.

Clive took her hand again, squeezed it, and let go.

Her mother's eyes, knowing and bright, settled on her again, and Poppy blushed.

Poppy Junior, from her haven in Mrs. Twigg's arms, made a gagging sound and vomited the undigested chocolate-covered cherries over a surprisingly large area. Cherries exploded onto walls and carpet, and dripped down Mrs. Twigg's coat, which, Poppy noticed now, she had never removed.

Poppy's mother said briskly, "Well, I think she'll be all right now, Mrs. Twigg. Let's you and I go downstairs and get you cleaned up. We'll take your dog into the laundry yard. You three can clean this up." She and Mrs. Twigg were gone in an instant.

Spock stepped forward and sniffed, with all the solemn gravitas of a sommelier, at a glob of the vomit, then recoiled. To his credit, Spock was not the least bit interested in eating any.

"Too bad Horatio isn't here," Poppy said and they all cracked up, for even Price knew all about the sublime Horatio.

A rag was found, the rug and wall were scrubbed, and hands were washed. In the kitchen Mummy and Mrs. Twigg, her coat hanging up, cleaned off, were chatting amiably about

Mrs. Twigg's former employer, a person of the previous generation, a member of a rival garden club, whom her mother had known only slightly.

In the kitchen Poppy's mother had already prepared a fresh pot of her favorite smoky brew. The Limoges was out. There were more cookies. A low arrangement of pussy willows now stood in the center of the table. Mrs. Twigg asked if they were from her garden and her mother admitted, no, she always bought them at the Philadelphia Flower Show. Mrs. Twigg nodded and said that she and her daughter attended the show for free, during off hours, because a neighbor was on the building maintenance crew of the giant facility. Clive joined the conversation, mentioning the orchids, this year's theme, and they all agreed that orchids should always be the theme. There was nothing else like them except maybe roses. Then conversation petered out and everyone took a sip of tea at the same time.

Clive met Poppy's eyes, asking, begging.

"I'm going to take Spock out," she announced, "five minutes, okay? Then we'll go."

Price, as she knew he would, slid his chair back. "I'll go with you."

Poppy asked Mrs. Twigg if she would like her to take Poppy Junior outside, but Mrs. Twigg shook her head, no.

Her mother's eyebrows shot up. "Poppy Junior?" she asked, ready laughter in her voice.

"Mrs. Twigg named her new dog after me," Poppy said with mock defiance.

"You are quite special to me, young lady," Mrs. Twigg said.

"Poppy is certainly unique," her mother said, looking directly at Poppy and smiling, so that the gap between her front teeth was visible.

Once they were outside Price said, "Ah, Poppy, no algorithm will ever capture you."

Poppy rolled her eyeballs. "That's true of everyone," she said.

"Sadly, not the case." Price spoke with dry authority and Poppy did not argue.

They stood on the bricks in the laundry yard, a familiar and comforting place where, when very little, they had played for hours under Sybil's watchful eye. The cool and damp air had a spicy, almost bitter smell from the interaction of moisture, rock, brick, moss, and dirt. Less than seventy years old, the yard with its buckled bricks, mossy walls, and rusted iron rings for the laundry lines seemed much older.

They strolled into the driveway and Price said, "Before we get to me, I am wondering how things are with you?"

"Why? Did Mummy say something?" Price did not answer, which meant she had.

Which way to go? They could keep walking straight into the vegetable garden or go around to where the car was parked. Spock chose for them and headed for the car.

Poppy looked sidelong at Price. He seemed very concentrated. When he felt her gaze, he said, "Poppy, I'm wondering what else you think there is?" His expression was gentle and quizzical, but he had his head tipped back and his brow furrowed, signs that he was serious.

"What do you mean?" Poppy said, hearing the defensiveness in her tone.

Price waved an arm. His voice took on an edge. "Do you have any idea how lucky you are to have met someone like Clive? Who loves you? Who 'gets' you? Do you know what my chances are of finding someone like that?"

Price went on, "And, to answer your question," his tone even sharper, "she already knew. She said she'd figured it out when I was quite small. 'The way you do things,' she said, whatever that means." By the way he hunched his shoulders, Poppy understood that he disliked the idea his mother had known all along.

"Well, she *is* your mother," Poppy said. "She couldn't exactly tell you, could she?"

Price rolled his shoulders. "No. She couldn't. She was very gracious," he said. "We kept on drinking our tea and eating cookies as if it was all very ordinary."

"Will you tell Daddy?"

Price shrugged. Their father was presently living in Indiana. Two years after leaving their mother he'd married a former student, a kindly, prosaic woman most of them liked well enough, almost better than their father. They'd heard rumors that he still roved, but they'd also heard that their stepmother was less tolerant than their own mother had been, and was forcing him to choose: quit philandering or he was out the door.

To Poppy, on a visit not so long ago, her father had referred to her half-siblings as "my children" with no apparent awareness that he was, by implication, excluding her. When she protested, "I'm your child too!" he'd frowned and said in a very annoyed tone of voice, "Context, Poppy. I meant nothing exclusionary. I consider you an adult now, or close enough."

"I'll always be your child, Daddy," she'd said. "That never changes."

Her father's expression had closed then, whether in anger or guilt or both, who could say?

Poppy now said to Price, "He'll say, 'Hmmm,' the way he always does when you tell him something he doesn't know how to respond to and then he'll quote something from Marcus Aurelius."

They laughed.

Price said, "Anyway, I can't see making a special trip for him. I don't think he'll care one way or the other."

"Isn't that good?" Poppy asked.

They were walking along the narrow stretch between the house and the main road above, where hundreds of daffodils bloomed among the scattered shrubs and beeches on the downward slope. The sun had set, but in the last glow of sunset, the yellows and whites of the flower petals were slightly phosphorescent.

"I don't know what I expected," Price said, "most of the time coming out is a huge shock for families. Yelling, doors slamming, wills changed. In my family, everyone says, 'Of course, that makes so much sense,' or 'I already knew.' There's no drama, no upset, just warm acceptance."

Poppy held her tongue. *It was a huge shock to me,* she wanted to say, but the words stuck in her throat. *I'm hurt you didn't tell me sooner.* "You're not disappointed, are you?"

"Not at all," he said, "I only hope people are being truthful."

The lights in the kitchen were on, and the window over the sink was a bright rectangle. Spock ran to the back of the car, figuring they were getting ready to go, but Poppy and Price turned onto a path snaking through the ivy into the deepening dusk of the woods opposite the front door. Here, on a slight rise, was the tree house, not a proper one built in a tree, but on four stilts that their mother had bought from FAO Schwarz for Silas and Cal and installed in this lightly wooded area between the house and the next property.

Without any discussion, they climbed; Poppy went first, carefully, but the ladder seemed sturdy enough. Price couldn't quite stand up under the gambrel roof and the kneewalls only came up to his mid-thigh. A few leaves were scattered about but the floor wasn't dirty, so they sat down.

Spock, left alone below, whined and scratched.

Poppy poked her head out to reassure him. "Hang on there, buddy. We won't be long." Sighing, Spock lay down.

"So," Price asked, "this test of Clive's?"

She explained about Clive's father.

They fell silent.

Poppy's heart pounded. "Can I ask you something?"

"Sure."

Not looking at him, she asked, "So why didn't you tell me sooner?"

Price sighed. "I knew you'd hate that I kept it from you. I don't know how to describe my internal life, Pops, but try to believe me when I say that even now I don't totally believe I am gay. That is, I am, and I know I am, I've known for fifteen years, but when I was twelve or so and I figured it out, I started checking everything I was going to say before I spoke to make sure I didn't give myself away. It's not like I consciously split myself apart, more that once I started I couldn't stop." He grimaced. "I like women much more than many gay men do. Almost enough. You wouldn't believe how many view women as barely human. I'm not like that."

"It's not unique to gay men," Poppy said drily. "Plenty of straight men don't like women much either, as I learned waiting tables. You wouldn't believe what I overheard and saw." As Price talked she was staring at a nail holding the sidewall to a post that had partially pulled out, splintering the wood. It didn't look structural.

"Clive's unusual, you know. He's amazingly uncomplicated. And he really loves you, Pops."

"It's not Clive I'm worried about. It's me."

Price said, "What? Why?" His surprise was genuine. She felt his attention focus.

"I never once in my life thought about marrying anybody, not until I met Clive. I'm afraid he'll get tired of me. I think it would be better if I had my own life more sorted out."

Price shook his head. "Your chances might be better than you think given that you are free of romantic illusions."

"Oh, I have plenty of illusions," Poppy said. "I was remembering our game while I was in the playroom." She picked at the splinters. "I feel like I'm still playing house. You know, we never played at having families. We lived alone. We never talked about what our jobs were. We went to them and came home, but I don't remember ever being specific. When we got bored, we tore down the houses and started over. We weren't committed to anything; it was very self-centered."

Price paused to consider. "I don't agree."

"So what were we doing?"

"We were making our own normal," Price said. "We were learning how to cooperate. Don't you remember how we fought all the time before Daddy left?"

"You were such a know-it-all," Poppy retorted.

"You were so easy to provoke." They grinned at each other. "But thank you for using the past tense."

"But why? Why did we bother?" Poppy made a face.

"We needed each other, Pops."

"Was that all?"

Price's voice was thoughtful. "At first, but that changed. You were a lot more fun to be with than I expected. I loved planning and carrying out those raids of ours on the kitchen. Remember your diversions? You'd set up these elaborate scenarios to distract Sybil or Mummy while I nabbed the cookies and drinks."

"Did I?"

"No one, not even Mom or Sybil, could ever resist; they fell for your ploys every time. Remember the one where everyone had to go look for that missing hamster in the basement? I nabbed so much food we couldn't eat it all."

Poppy started at that. She had found that hamster, dead in a bucket, sometime a few days earlier and had buried it by herself, telling no one. That's what gave her the idea, but Price didn't need to know that detail.

He went on, "You were so convincing. It was just like your plays, like you just knew what we needed. Those characters you gave us? Remember UnGrogg who was always trying to make trouble and was furious when everything he tried always turned out for the good? He was my favorite character of yours ever."

"UnGrogg," Poppy said musing, "I haven't thought of him in years." She did remember how much Price had loved that role. An image of him cackling with abandon as he galloped around the stage arose; he was wearing a cape he'd made himself onto which he'd sewn odds and ends, the inside wrappers of chewing gum, bottle caps, tin foil. The cape had made a delicious rattling sound.

"You were eleven. How did you come up with that idea?"

"I don't know," Poppy said. "Maybe I was smarter then. Grown-ups were always talking to me about learning the difference between making things up and lying. That it was great I was so creative but blah blah blah. You know I was terrible at those kinds of boundaries. I probably still am."

"You could do worse," Price said. "A person can hide behind boundaries and never live. I was doing that."

"Well, I worry that Clive is going to get tired of me. I get tired of being me," Poppy said. "I'm the opposite of your UnGrogg."

"You don't make trouble, Poppy. You do seem to attract . . . I don't know . . . maybe the opposite—you don't usually avoid confrontation."

Poppy was unconvinced. "I'm avoiding it now? And that's supposed to be comforting?"

"Maybe not comforting, but helpful?" Price said. "We'd better get back. Clive is at the end of his patience." Tolerantly, he added, "Promise me you won't do anything spectacularly stupid? I expect marriage is a gamble, but your chances look good to me."

Poppy climbed down ahead of Price, her throat tight with emotion. When she stepped on the ground, Spock, feeling her mood, leaned his head against her leg and Poppy bent down to inhale the musty smell of dog, a soothing and grounding perfume to her.

"I'll try," she said. "I really will try."

She put Spock in the car. The spring air had turned chilly with the sun gone. They turned to walk toward the kitchen, as Price knew she did not like to use the front door.

"Do you have someone?" Poppy asked tentatively.

Even in the half-dark she knew she had asked a painful question.

"No," he said. Then more quietly, "no."

The two Prices have spoken, she thought. He's still checking, even with me. Poppy felt something settle on her shoulders that made her want to fling her arms around her brother and hold him tight and keep him safe, but he wasn't the sort of person you did that to.

The entry light over the front door went on and the door opened. Time to go.

NIGHT

Poppy's mother, in the vanguard, was declaring, "Don't think you're going anywhere without giving me a hug and a kiss."

Poppy, mid-embrace, inhaled the scent of her mother's familiar lotion and something else, close and animal, which meant "comfort" and "mother." Her mother was murmuring, "I'm so glad about the results of Clive's test."

Disarmed, Poppy whispered back, "We're so relieved."

Price's good-bye embrace was, as usual, bony and awkward and Poppy only managed to kiss the edge of his ear. When they stood back, he raised his eyebrows while tipping his head sideways and she read, *Don't screw up.*

On Lancaster Avenue, she pulled into the shopping center with the discount pet store. Spock and Clive remained in the car while Mrs. Twigg and Poppy and Poppy Junior went in to buy food, treats, a suitable bowl, collar, and leash. Poppy chose a squeaky plush pig toy as a present for her namesake. The store was quiet and Poppy Junior shivered under the harsh lighting. They did not linger over the leashes and collars, taking the one with daisies on purple over the yellow dog bones on blue. By the time they got to the check-out counter, Mrs. Twigg was drooping. She had pulled out some cash from her purse, but Poppy shook her head. It was a measure of how tired Mrs. T was that she barely protested.

"I never meant to keep you out so late," Poppy said apologetically, "it's the least I can do."

Outside, the cool evening air revived Mrs. Twigg. She said, "I've enjoyed meeting your fiancé and family, and seeing your childhood home. You know so much about me, now I know more about you."

Poppy had several responses she wanted to make, among them, "He's not my fiancé!" and "I hardly know you at all," and was glad she hadn't when Mrs. Twigg added, "Your brother reminds me of my son, Michael. Such a mannerly young man, and your mother, she is a fine woman."

Mrs. Twigg's comment about her mother did not surprise Poppy—she undoubtedly knew all there was to know about women like her. She guessed too, that what Mrs. Twigg meant was that her mother probably was a decent person to work for, fair and conscientious and kind. Sometimes Poppy was envious of her mother's assumptions, not because they had any merit, but because her own generation had given up those certainties. She had had advantages, yes, good dentistry and a good education, but those only got you so far.

What did surprise her was Mrs. Twigg comparing Price to her son, Michael.

Poppy Junior was snuggled tight against Mrs. Twigg's chest. Clive got out to open the back. Poppy noted, as she put the bags in, that Spock had moved back to the middle seat, but neither Mrs. Twigg nor Poppy Junior appeared to mind.

Clive offered to drive and Poppy gratefully handed over the keys.

Traffic was light and in a few minutes they were swinging onto Belmont Avenue, where soon the trees would leaf out, giving this part of the route an almost rural feeling. She leaned back in the passenger seat. Mrs. Twigg wasn't the only tired person. Clive drove sedately, letting the other cars pass, red taillights growing smaller like vanishing embers. As they entered the city, they made increasingly tight turns onto ever narrower streets.

Then the full import of her mother's last remark to her slammed into place.

Her mother had known about the test!

Which meant that someone (Clive!) had told her. When? The Flower Show. They had spent the whole day together. How had Mummy extracted the information out of him? Not that difficult, Clive wasn't secretive; all she'd had to do was ask the right question. How did she know to ask?

Poppy glanced at Clive, but he was oblivious, concentrating on navigating the increasingly narrow streets in the huge car. They all agreed, her siblings and herself, that their mother had powers, or maybe all attentive mothers knew more about you than you did. Imagine waiting all that time to see what Price would do. And what did she really think? Her mother's cronies were almost all divorced or widowed women, and were surprisingly tolerant. They all knew who was queer among them. They were the ones, of both genders, who had never married, and the men were always available to squire to the theater or be an extra man at a dinner party and the women often lived alone or even discreetly with another spinster.

At Mrs. Twigg's there was nowhere to pull over, so Clive kept the car running, ready to circle the block. Poppy carried the bags. When they got to the door, Mrs. Twigg put Poppy

Junior, in her new collar and leash, down and pulled out her key. The curtains were pulled shut but Poppy could hear the murmur of the TV and see the gleam of a light. "Alma's at work tonight. We do that even when no one's home," Mrs. Twigg said.

As they stepped over the threshold a rich aroma of something hearty washed over them. "Alma left me a hot dinner," said Mrs. Twigg happily, "I told her I might be a while." The moment that Mrs. Twigg let Poppy Junior off the leash, the tiny dog began running about inspecting the room. When Poppy returned from taking the bags into the kitchen, she found Mrs. Twigg sunk in a chair, with Poppy Junior in her lap. "You remember to eat that good food," Poppy said as she left.

Before putting the car in gear, Clive slung a friendly arm along the back of the seat and tickled her shoulder. "Alone at last with your menfolk," he said.

Poppy extended her seat belt to snuggle closer to him. In the back Spock flopped around discontentedly. His towel was in the way back.

"Well, darling," Clive said cheerfully, "here's your chance to say 'Home, Jeeves.'" He'd turned on the heat and the car was warm. He was in shirtsleeves and his strong male scent surrounded her, a reminder of the stresses of the day.

"Does Jeeves cook?"

"Jeeves can do anything, but we can give him the night off and eat out."

"Once I get home, I won't want to go out again. I'm too tired to cook and too tired to walk anywhere."

"There's in, by way of takeout," Clive suggested.

Poppy agreed to that.

What she would like best would be to eat a bowl of cereal and crawl into bed alone in a darkened, silent room. *This is a piece of marriage I'm not sure about. The way you are always with the same person.* She had seen, in the restaurant, those older couples who had nothing to say to one another anymore. That boredom and lack of interest was almost more frightening to her than the couples that clashed publicly.

The prolonged intimacy and exposure, the squashing and rearranging of moods and impulses to accommodate or not hurt the feelings of another daunted Poppy. There were situations she got herself into that she had no idea how to get out of. There were days when she was in a fey mood, her mind unsettled, when she had no idea how to handle herself, much less someone else.

Even more importantly she had no idea why, today, it had been so difficult to give Clive the attention he deserved. This could not augur well for their future, could it, that her own heart had stubbornly resisted?

Why was she so bothered that Clive had told her mother about the test? After all, this was his secret to tell others. Was it that her mother was the only person she had been tempted to confide in? Was she jealous?

All the same Clive could have *told* her that Mummy knew. She would have liked having someone to talk to. It might have helped her focus more on Clive.

She was being too quiet, and Poppy could feel Clive's cheerfulness ebbing. He removed his arm and said, "Poppy? Are you having one of your 'things'?"

"Well, maybe, sort of," she said softly, "yes," squeezing her eyes shut.

Granted, Price showing up today had happened out of the blue and Clive had readily agreed to help him, but Poppy could have made different arrangements with Mrs. Twigg. She could have insisted on dropping her at home before heading for the suburbs. They could have gone shopping later.

Keeping her eyes shut, Poppy continued saying nothing. If she kept quiet sometimes these dark moods passed quickly before the wrong words escaped, treacherous and sticky, and making everything worse. She put a hand on Clive's thigh, hoping that would be answer enough for now.

Soon they were crossing over the Spring Garden Street Bridge into Philadelphia proper. The art museum, lit up and glowing, loomed. In five minutes they would be home. They stopped at a light in the great serpentine curve that Spring Garden Street makes before returning to a straight course toward the Delaware River. Spock moved restlessly; he always knew exactly where they were, and no doubt was anticipating his long-overdue dinner.

As they waited at the light, Clive asked, "Poppy?" Choosing words carefully, he asked, "What is the matter? What is upsetting you? Can you explain?"

With forced neutrality Poppy said, "It's stupid, but I was surprised you told Mummy about your test. I thought we weren't telling anyone."

"I didn't mean to," he said, "but you know how she is. We were in a line waiting to buy pussy willows."

"How?" Poppy asked, skeptical but amused, "how did you get from pussy willows to heart valves?"

"We started talking about places where pussy willows grew when we were children. There were loads in the back of the graveyard where my father was buried, near a stream where everyone went to fill up their watering cans. After church my mother liked to 'tidy up' around Dad's headstone, and in the spring we kids would pick pussy willows to take home, and we'd put some around him too. You know, if the conditions are right, if you stick a pussy willow twig in the ground it'll take root. By the end of summer there was a little green fence around Dad. The fellow who kept the place mowed would always pull them all up before winter, but we think he watered them in the summer. Your mother interrupted me to ask if I knew whether I had the same problem my father had, if I'd been tested, so I had to tell her I was looking into it. If we hadn't stopped for the pussy willows, I wouldn't have said anything."

"She always buys bundles of them," Poppy said. "She's mad for pussy willows."

"Are you mad at me?" he asked.

"No," she said firmly, "how can I be? Who can resist my mother?"

This glimpse of Clive and his sisters in their Sunday best was achingly sweet: she could see his sisters in their patent leather shoes and white socks, the boys in polished oxfords and corduroy trousers (she'd seen pictures), careful not to get anything dirty but being with and taking care of their father in this way, creating a living green wall to protect and shelter him.

Clive's story shifted the dark and she felt better. Stories did that, woke her up to all the wonders going on outside her closed-off self.

As they drove down their own street the sky above them was visible because the trees were still bare. Once the trees were leafed out the street would become a glowing green tunnel lit from underneath by the street lamps.

Clive let out a whoop. A parking space big enough for the behemoth was right in front of their house. He pulled up and backed in smoothly and turned off the car, grinning.

"Today went fine, Poppy. Going out to your Mom's was good, getting out of the city, fresh air. I'm glad we could help Price and your friend, Mrs. Twigg, and Poppy Junior. I've never seen a happier couple."

"I can't help feeling guilty," Poppy admitted. "I assumed you'd be fine. I never worried at all. I didn't get it until *after*, in that garden."

"After my father died, I felt guilty whenever I forgot about him, which being a fourteen-year-old I did frequently. It's human nature, Pops, don't perplex yourself."

A word. Perplex. *If I was a fish, he dropped exactly the right bait to catch me.* She leaned across the huge expanse of seat to give him a kiss.

"If you really feel guilty," he added, "you can devote the rest of the evening to me."

"I can do that," Poppy said.

Clive climbed out of the car and opened the tailgate to get his briefcase. After checking that all the windows were rolled up, Poppy got out and opened the street-side door for Spock, got her own bag, reached into the back to throw Spock's towel forward into the middle for tomorrow. On the sidewalk Spock stretched, and then got busy sprinkling the area around their tree to let any interested parties know he was "at home." Clive had left the door ajar and Spock went in on his own.

Poppy trudged up the steps, pausing on the stoop. Only ten hours ago she'd stood here, the day fresh. Why were the beginning and end of each day so different? *We are bound,* she thought, *by our experience of day and night. We think of everything as having a beginning and ending, as being new or old, and of ourselves as fresh or fatigued. Out in the void, there is no night and day, no beginning and no ending. Nothing but a profound and indifferent silence.*

Clive was studying the take-out menu and Spock's bowl was clunking against the baseboards as he chowed down his dinner. All Clive needed was the phone number because even when they spent a half-hour studying their choices on that menu they ordered the same dishes in the end: won-ton soup, dumplings, vegetarian egg rolls, chicken fried noodles, beef with snow peas or asparagus, and extra brown rice.

By the time their dinner arrived they'd be in comfortable clothing, installed on the sofa ready to watch a show that Clive had recorded off the TV (carefully erasing the ads) on the new VHS system he'd bought with his Christmas bonus. Already they had a good collection: *Around the World in Eighty Days, Journey to the Center of the Earth, Thunderball,* and a lot of *Star Trek.* Not long after that they would be naked in bed.

As she hung up her scarf and jacket and fished the containers that had held her meager lunch out of the canvas bag, she was thinking again of the cushion-and-sheet houses she had made with Price. Price saying, "What else do you think there is?" Was it practice for this? This is what people do. Make homes, have families. She would get better at it. *They* would get better at it together.

After feeding Spock and while waiting for the take-out to arrive, Poppy went up to their room to change, but soon found herself in her study. There was her own journal that she didn't write in often enough abandoned on her desk.

She turned on the light, picked up a pen and sat down. She'd write something in it right now.

What a day! Thankfully, almost over.

She made lists, while her mind was fresh: the names of all the people she had talked to and dogs she had walked today. The places she had been, from the shelter to the airport, and including different areas of her mother's house, the garden, playroom, the kitchen, and the tree house.

Then she wrote: *What I choose to write about these people, dogs, and places reflects back to me who I am and what is important to me. I can't hold on to any insights into myself and I can't get away from myself. Many of these people said things to me about myself that I don't* . . . What was the right word? *Believe? See? Understand?* Like Price's comments about her plays.

Poppy was so absorbed that she jumped when Clive called up, "Food's here!" She hadn't heard the doorbell. Her sweatshirt had deep pockets and she slipped the journal into one of them. Even though she doubted she'd have the energy or the privacy to write more tonight, she wanted to keep the journal close. Writing had calmed her. Perhaps that was what, most of all, Boswell's journals were for him, a way to soothe and sort out the wild tumult in his mind.

While they ate they watched an episode of *Star Trek*. When their plates had nothing left on them but sauce and bits of drying-out brown rice, they both leaned back. This was an episode where Spock, Uhuru, and Kirk fall into an alternate universe where ambition and cruelty rule supreme. As with most episodes in the series, the story was thought provoking, maddening, touching, and, like all good science fiction, amazingly prescient.

"I wish they'd make more *Star Trek*," Clive moaned. He said this every time they watched an episode.

Poppy, replete with the bloated Chinese-food feeling, said nothing. In a few minutes she would take Spock out one last time, rinse a few dishes, put the leftovers away, and they'd go to bed. Right now she couldn't move.

The phone rang. "Ugh," Poppy said.

"Let the answering machine get it," Clive said.

"It's probably Price."

"Look at the number before you pick up." They had a new answering machine that showed the number of whoever was calling.

She frowned as she looked at the number: familiar, but not *that* familiar, but Irene and Millicent had the same exchange.

"Let's listen," Clive said.

They waited. Poppy was disgusted by the length of her recorded greeting. "You have reached Poppy's Dog Walking Service and also the home of . . . etcetera . . ." BEEP.

After a pause a frantic male voice came on. "Hello, hello? Oh damn! This is terrible! I was *really* hoping to get you, Poppy. Phil Burns, here, Irene's neighbor. I'm worried about her . . . the kitchen lights never came on and the dog is barking nonstop . . . Before I call 911, which I *know* she would *hate*, I thought I'd see if you could come down and have a look."

The novelty of hearing Mr. Burns calling himself "Phil" and saying "damn" launched Poppy off the sofa.

"Hello, hello? Sorry, Mr. Burns, my hands were wet. Doing dishes."

"Oh thank God you're there, Poppy. I'm terribly worried. I'm positive she's home. Irene, I mean. I've telephoned several times and all that happens is the dog barks even louder. We've talked about exchanging keys, but we never have got around to it."

"Are you sure she's home?"

"Positive. Molly saw her earlier when she was out with Ollie, and you know, they both like that PBS mystery show, on tonight, which they discussed. Furthermore, Penelope never barks like that. *Never*."

Poppy felt a sort of coolness in her extremities, as if her body heat were retreating to some central core to harness energy.

To Clive, she whispered, "Something's happened to Irene. It's her neighbor."

Mr. Burns was still talking. ". . . I hate to ask you this, but could you come over and check? I really don't want to call 911. Since I don't have a key they'll probably wreck her door with a crowbar or some damn thing. Even if she is badly hurt, she'd never forgive me!"

"We can be there in under fifteen," Poppy said, raising her eyebrows at Clive, who nodded, resigned.

After Mr. Burns hung up, Clive said, "He should have called 911."

"You don't know Irene."

"I know her as well as I ever want to," Clive retorted. "Let's go, Miss Nightingale."

Poppy felt a slight pang at abandoning the miracle parking spot so soon, but it couldn't be helped. Clive drove and as Poppy put on her seat belt she felt the bulk of her journal in her pocket. An hour ago she had thought the day was almost over, that she'd have a few minutes to capture more details from the day.

Had Mr. Burns called a half-hour later they would have ignored the ringing phone and would not have listened to the message until the morning.

They bickered briefly over what route to take, but Clive was driving. He reminded her that they had recently ruled "driver's choice."

"Go any way you want, then," Poppy said, "just get us there."

Ten minutes later, Clive beached the car on the sidewalk, flipping the blinkers on. Poppy leapt out, door key in hand.

Mr. Burns was waiting for her on his stoop and ran over. His hair was mussed and he was in khakis, sweatshirt, and espadrilles. "I apologize for disturbing you," he said, "but I am so relieved you were home. This door, you know? It's original, she says, if some fireman hacked it open, she'd sue the city and god forbid what she would do to me."

Poppy said, "Don't worry, Mr. Burns. I'm here now." She turned and stooped a little to get the key in the lock.

"Really, Poppy, you should call me Phil, please," he said.

Poppy could hear Penelope barking somewhere in the house, a steady and repetitive sound, rife with despair and fear. Then she was in.

The alarm was not turned on. Irene had had an attempted break-in and never went out in the day or night or to bed without turning it on. Her stomach clutched.

She called out, "Irene?" Her voice sounded thin and wavery. She thought she heard something, a thump, a groan, maybe? Penelope was making too much noise. *Upstairs,* Poppy thought, that was where the barking was coming from.

She had a vision of Irene naked, having fallen in her tub. Nothing on earth would humiliate Irene more than a rescue squad much less a *neighbor* seeing her in such a predicament. Worse even than the police battering down her precious door.

She turned and said firmly to Mr. Burns and Clive, who was right behind him, "I'm going up first . . . I'll call you when I see what's going on." She took the stairs two at a time, calling out "Irene?"

And there she was, on the floor, in the little hall between her library and the stairs, lying flat on her back, fully dressed. The small oriental runner was rumpled up against the bannisters. Irene opened her blue eyes and said almost inaudibly, "I knew you'd come. I slipped on that damned rug. Mathilde always said I would. I believe I've broken my hip."

Both men had already run halfway up the stairs, but Mr. Burns immediately retreated, saying he'd call for the ambulance. Penelope flew into Poppy's arms and she sat down, letting the frantic dog lick her face.

Clive moved past Poppy and knelt down next to Irene. "You need anything? Water."

"Penelope needs to go out," Irene said hoarsely. "Yes, I could use some water. Poppy, you stay." Except for the faintness of her voice she spoke calmly, as if they were sitting in the library having tea.

Clive took Penelope.

"Come closer," Irene whispered, "I've been lying here so long that I . . . I let go. I'm lying in a pool of pee."

"I can't move you," Poppy whispered back, "the ambulance people have to do that. They won't mind."

"But *I* mind," said Irene, closing her eyes, and Poppy could feel Irene's anger and frustration blow like a hot wind.

"I'll get a towel to mop up what I can. I can't move you at all though, that would be dangerous."

"You'll come with me to the hospital? You'll bring my things? A change of clothes for coming home, clean undies? A robe? My hairbrush? My insurance card is in my purse. I'll need that." Her voice grew ever softer and Poppy understood how much pain she was in, how very fatigued she was.

"Yes, of course," Poppy said. "We'll stay with you until you are settled and we'll take care of Penelope, no worries, not about anything. Shall I call your sons?"

Irene grimaced. "Don't waste your time." Then she said, "Their numbers are on my emergency sheet in the kitchen. But there's no rush."

Mr. Burns came partway up the stairs and said, "An ambulance is on the way." Poppy could only see the top of his head and was impressed by his tactfulness, " . . . so I'll wait for them down by the door." She had managed to give Irene a few more sips of water before the EMTs came bounding up the stairs and swept Poppy aside.

In Irene's room, she found a canvas bag on a chair, dumped the contents onto the bed, and then started to gather what Irene had asked for, deciding on loose linen trousers and a button-down shirt, both blue, one light the other dark, several pairs of clean underwear, two nightgowns, socks. In the closet she found a velvety quilted bed jacket in blue and a light-weight cashmere bathrobe in peach, and stuffed them both in the bag, along with some satiny slippers. In the bathroom, other than toothbrush and paste, she had no idea what Irene needed. There was a surprising amount of makeup. Opening a few drawers she found an empty toiletry bag and randomly, as she did not use makeup herself, picked out a face cream, eyebrow liner and pencil, and some blusher and put those in along with the toothpaste and brush. Hairbrush. Comb. Hand cream caught her eye and she put that in. Beside the sink there were several bottles of pills. She swept them all into the toiletry bag. What else? Irene's lipstick was probably in her handbag. She'd need to find that too.

She ran downstairs and found Clive and Mr. Burns stand-ing on the stoop, watching the EMTs finish loading Irene into the ambulance. Poppy was relieved to hear that they were taking her to the "good" hospital nearby; they weren't all the same.

Clive went to get the car out of the parking space and Poppy went back into the kitchen. She found the insurance card and lipstick in Irene's purse. After that she went to the phone list.

What were her sons' names? Theodore, Martin, and Law-rence. But only Theodore lived somewhere nearby out in horse country. Unionville, maybe. She found his name.

The ambulance left as she picked up the phone. As she dialed, Poppy glanced at the kitchen clock. Only a little past ten. Not that late. Poppy took a deep breath, reminding herself this really was an emergency.

After three rings a woman answered, clearly put out. She asked for Mr. Childress. Theodore. "You want Theodore Childress? Why? Who are you?"

Poppy said, "It's about his mother. She's been taken to the hospital. I'm . . . well, I'm a friend of hers. Her neighbor called me because I have a key."

"All right, I'll get him," said the woman, less aggressive, but no more friendly. Poppy heard her shout, "Teddy? Phone for you!" After that she must have covered the receiver with her hand, because all Poppy heard was murmurs for what seemed like a long time.

When Teddy came on the line, Poppy started to tell him what had happened, but he interrupted her, demanding, "Explain to me *who* you are, exactly? And *why* you have a key to my mother's house?"

Poppy blinked and began to explain. After half a minute, Teddy interrupted again saying, "Fine, fine, okay, I get who you are. So, what happened?" He listened, his impatience palpable. She told him the name of the hospital where Irene had been taken and that she planned to stop there before going home to make sure Irene was being looked after properly. She would also look after the dog.

Theodore, or Teddy, then made an effort to be friendlier. Gruffly, he thanked her for "having the situation" under control. Those were the words he used. Twice he asked for the name of the hospital, then said he'd call there first thing in the morning, and hung up. She had a feeling he would not call his brothers.

She stood there a moment, receiver in hand, but there was no time to think about *that* conversation. She had already told Mr. Burns that they would take Penelope, and Clive had taken her bed and food out when he went out again. She heard the beep of the Vista Cruiser horn, put Penelope on the leash, picked up the bags, turned on the alarm, and after locking up carefully behind her went out to the waiting car. Mr. Burns was standing by the driver's window talking to Clive and she said to him, "I'm going to make a spare key for you tomorrow. I'll poke it through your mail slot, okay?"

"Did you get hold of family?"

"Sort of," Poppy said. "Thank you, Mr. Burns."

Mr. Burns laughed affably and said, "I have to thank you both. Please, call me Phil." As they pulled away, he called out, "Let us know how she is and if there's anything we can do to help. She's a grand old thing."

"She doesn't deserve them as neighbors," Poppy said. "They don't even *get* that she finds them boring."

"Or, maybe they do," Clive said, "and they don't mind."

Poppy was relieved that Clive did not question her plan to stay until Irene was properly settled in a bed. They agreed that Clive would drop her off at the hospital, take Penelope back to their house, then come back supplied with books, a deck of cards, snacks: whatever a person needs for what might be a long sit in a hospital.

"You don't have to come back," she said, "I could come home in a cab."

"What else would I do?"

"Get some sleep?"

He laughed. "That's not what I want."

At the entrance to the ER, Poppy thought, from the phone call to now there had been little need for discussion, each one simply doing the next task that needed to be done. *We'd be good parents.* Not a thought Poppy particularly welcomed, but this was recognition of a kind of biological rightness between them, and this realization swept through her as she watched the oblong taillights of the car swing around a corner and out of sight.

At the intake desk Poppy lied, saying she was a grandchild, then pulled Irene's wallet out of the purse she had brought and gave the admissions person the insurance card. Once the paperwork was done they let Poppy go into one of those narrow curtained alcoves in Emergency where she found Irene lying very still, eyes shut, the lids blue, and her skin waxy. An IV was attached to her arm. Her chest rose and fell steadily, which was reassuring. There was also a clip on one of her fingers that attached her to a monitor that made little chirps and noises to accompany various graph lines marching across the screen.

This was one of those places where time ceased to pass in the usual way. Here they would wait. Doctors and nurses would come and go and then they would wait until eventually a decision was made or they came to the top of the list or however it worked.

The last time Poppy had been in an ER was with a college friend who'd had an asthma attack after eating something she didn't even know she was allergic to. The ER techs had attended to her friend immediately, giving her adrenaline, but subsequently kept her in one of these alcoves for about five hours of "observation" before they let her leave.

Shifting in the plastic chair, Poppy felt the hard surface of her journal against her side again and was also reminded that she was wearing clothes she would not normally leave the house wearing. Who cared? She was warm and comfortable and she had brought something to do. She went out to the nurse's desk where the woman on duty grudgingly let her have a ballpoint pen.

Opening the journal, she looked at the lists she had made earlier and began writing slowly, with hesitations, but then gradually more intently and rapidly. She wrote, soothed by the white noise that seemed to flow in one continuous hypnotic wave—machines beeping, faraway chatter at the nurse's station, the squeak of rubber-soled shoes or gurney wheels, the calm broken by an occasional groan or cry, like a submerged log briefly surfacing. She had gotten as far as Doctor Croydon's waiting room when she looked up to see Irene's eyes on her. "It's very kind of you, dear girl, but you don't have to stay."

"I'm staying," Poppy said. Irene closed her eyes and drifted off. Irene stayed asleep and Poppy thought there must be some kind of painkiller in the intravenous pouch.

At last orderlies came to wheel Irene away for x-rays and whatever came after that.

The aide directed Poppy to a corner in the main hall designated for families with patients in the ER. "We'll keep you informed about your grandma, but you won't see her again until she's in a room and that could be a long time, depending on the break, and who's available. She'll get a bed, though, we're not full tonight." As they walked together, it struck Poppy that the fact that hospitals always had to have technicians and doctors present to do x-rays and set broken bones, night and day, is a feature of civilization that is all too easy to take for granted.

The ER waiting room was nothing more than a remote corner of the immense main entrance hall, cordoned off with potted plants and sturdy partitions for a pretense at privacy. A placard near the entrance read, "E.R. Waiting Room Only. Please be respectful." She had her choice of seats as the waiting area was empty, and she chose one where she would be able to see Clive when he returned.

This huge lobby had the prayerful hush of a cathedral as well as the restless coming-and-going feeling of a train station—she felt very aware of herself as a one *very* small person. The atmosphere was not conducive to writing and Poppy's thoughts wandered. How many times had she passed by these windows walking or driving around the city? A hundred or more? She had often glanced at the people sitting where she now was. Clive was taking a long time, but maybe Penelope was upset.

Immense windows looked out into the darkness, the orange halos around the street lamps, the flare of passing headlamps, and across the street, inside the parking garage, bits of reflective plastic glowed red and yellow on the parked cars. Outside the night was taking over, inside the hospital was a hive, less busy at night but never completely still or quiet.

The magazines on the tables weren't the sort she could read ("Lose 5 lbs and Eat All You Want!!!," "Fifty Ways to Add a Water Feature to Your Garden," "Life after 'Dallas'—Will It Be Worth Living?").

After a time her thoughts settled and she pulled the journal out along with the pen she had not returned. Trying to capture even a fragment of this day was impossible, there was too much of it, the most one person could ever do was catch a moment here and there, a flash, a ripple. She had a feeling that she mostly noticed and remembered the details that fit into what she already recognized and expected. To go beyond those self-imposed limitations to find out something new was a struggle.

While she was still in the PhD program Poppy had, whenever she needed inspiration, requested to see random pages from the Boswell manuscripts. She would sit in the rare books room, wearing the little white cotton gloves, the papers before her. There was the ink, which Jamie himself had dipped in the inkwell, brown and faded on the paper, itself in varying states of disintegration. She would stare at the paper, at the ink, willing James Boswell, the living being who had sharpened quills, dipped the pen nibs and had written, blotted and written some more, to be *present* for her. All she needed was one instant of connection. She wanted the man to come alive, stout, dark-haired, ordinary looking—his best feature his dark intelligent eyes and his best attribute a quick wit.

Perhaps her professor was right. She did not have the scholarly temperament. Any more than Boswell was suited to be a soldier. She wasn't seeking answers to dry questions, she was seeking illumination, some insight into what drove a person.

Nor was she at all interested in imitating Boswell by attempting to write up as much of her life as she could find time for. How he had found the time or the energy to write so much about himself and still run off to see friends, whores, and hangings mystified her, although surely it helped that he had never had to cook or clean or shop. He had barely captured more than a tiny part of every day even so.

Two women pushed out of the ER doors, led by the same aide who had assisted her. One of the women, the younger one, was doubled over crying. The aide talked to the other woman, who nodded. Their sorrow was so intense and so immediate, so *private*, that Poppy stuffed the journal into her pocket and strode off into the large hall.

After using the bathroom she walked up and down the atrium hall a few times, until the person at the reception desk looked at her disapprovingly. As she headed back to the waiting area she saw Clive, walking rapidly, head down, carrying a canvas bag.

"Price called," Clive said, "that's what took me so long. He had a lot to say. He's changed his flight to early afternoon and he'll come in early and go around with you."

The waiting area had more people in it now. The sad pair were quiet, the younger woman's eyes were closed, her head on the shoulder of her comforter, who, to Poppy, appeared to be a person who knew how to be endlessly patient while waiting for news that was not going to be good. A couple maybe ten or fifteen years older than themselves sat in a corner; she was knitting and he had a book; they looked calm and resigned to a long night. Clive and Poppy found their own place to sit, equidistant from the others, and Poppy rummaged in the bag to see what Clive had brought. Peanut butter and jelly. She was hungry.

Eventually a different aide came to say a bed was being prepared. Then the resident orthopedic surgeon appeared and explained that Irene's was the simplest hip fracture, and that hers was not bad, only one step up from a hairline. He'd put in two "nails," he said, and Poppy tried not to wince. Grandma should be on her feet for a little walk by tomorrow afternoon. As he explained further, saying grandmother this and grandmother that, Poppy felt very uncomfortable that she was pretending to be a close relative.

After 2 a.m., when Irene was in a bed, Poppy and Clive went up. Clive collapsed in an armchair by the empty bed near the window. Irene was fast asleep in the bed by the bathroom, thoroughly knocked out by pain meds. She looked ghastly, disheveled and pale, her skin like parchment. Irene would hate people seeing her like this. Good thing she was asleep.

Someone bustled in from the corridor, "May I help you? Are you the family?"

Poppy spun around dumbfounded. She knew that deep, no-nonsense voice.

"Alma?"

"Poppy!" Alma exclaimed. "Is this your grandma?"

Poppy shook her head, glad to tell the truth, and began to explain about the lack of family; Alma frowned as she listened.

Then Alma nodded. "That happens a lot more than it should. Don't worry, honey, I won't give you away. You do provide full service, I'll say that much." She chuckled. "I talked to Mama on my break and she told me all about getting Junior, and going out to the country and meeting your mama and your brother and your fiancé." She glanced in Clive's direction and he gave her a feeble wave.

Her eyes settled on the stuffed canvas bag in Poppy's hands and she asked, "Those her things? Put them in that little cubbyhole closet. Did you bring her medications?"

Poppy nodded.

"Good girl," Alma said. "I'll take those. She got all her marbles?"

"Yes, and a few extra." Poppy could have laughed, for all they did not look the least bit alike, Alma sounded exactly like Mrs. Twigg.

"Good. The lady can tell me herself when she wakes up what she's gotta take, so I can check she really knows."

Poppy handed over the medications to Alma, who read the labels and wrote notes on the chart while she was hanging up the nightgowns, shirt, and robe on hangars, folding the trousers and underwear to put on the higher shelf. The makeup bag and toiletries went on the bedside table where Irene would see them first thing.

Clive had slumped down in the armchair, eyes closed.

When Alma was finished with the medications she said, "I'll be a few minutes, then you two can head home, okay?" Alma gave the privacy curtain a yank and then disappeared inside.

"Clive?"

He opened his eyes, blankly as if he didn't know where he was. Then focused on her.

"Why don't you go get the car," Poppy said. "I'll be right behind you. Alma wants to have a quick word when she's done here."

"Five minutes," he said groggily.

Poppy waited in the corridor. The first thing she said when Alma appeared was, "I didn't mean to keep your mother out so late. I hope she's okay."

Alma raised an eyebrow. "Honey, she had the time of her life, meeting your folks and seeing where you did your growing up." She looked Poppy up and down then. "Tell the truth, I haven't known what to think about you, you and my mama, thick as thieves. All Miss Poppy this and Miss Poppy that. I'm grateful, but you know, you're not family. And now naming that itty-bitty dog, Poppy Junior," Alma went on firmly, "so I say to her, what if you are insulted, and she says you know better. And . . ."

After a hesitation, Alma dropped her voice and said. "She told me . . . she says how your brother reminded her of . . . of . . . her son, my brother . . . Michael."

Everything came to a full stop.

"He was the nicest boy and then the nicest, biggest-hearted man ever lived. We all loved him, you couldn't *not* love Mike."

Poppy held her breath. "What happened?"

Alma's face turned hard. "He was beaten up for being . . ." she turned away, "too different. A black and . . . the other thing too, you know." She couldn't even say the word. "They said his army squad never meant to hurt him so bad, it was a prank that got out of hand. All a big mistake." Alma had to pause to take a breath, "He was our Mike, our joy. We knew about his ways, but we none of us spoke of it. My mama, she wants you to pay attention to your brother. Watch over him, pray for him, that he be safe. My brother never should have gone in the service, but he wanted the money for school."

Alma's hazel brown eyes blazed with fury and sorrow. Alma's white uniform was so white it was blinding.

What else do you think there is? What are you waiting for? she heard Price saying.

Poppy, staring, must have looked so stricken that she alarmed Alma.

"Honey? Poppy?"

"I'm all right. Thank you, thank you, for explaining," Poppy whispered, and they embraced, first cautiously and then more warmly and fully.

The miraculous parking space was still there.

"That's three times," Clive commented. "I parked here when I dropped off the dogs too."

"We won't get this spot again for years," Poppy said mournfully, "all our parking karma used up in one day."

"You could shift the odds and get a car that only requires one parking space instead of two," Clive said deadpan.

She punched him lightly in the shoulder. "Wise guy."

Much as Poppy would have liked to go straight up to bed, both dogs were waiting expectantly at the door; Penelope subdued but alert and Spock visibly anxious. They would be reassured if she took them out. Normally Poppy waited on the stoop while Spock did his business, but Penelope couldn't be off the leash, even with no one around. They went down to the sidewalk.

The air was cool but not wintry and Poppy could feel the fizz of spring bubbling upward in the trees and shrubs. The dogs' nails were loud on the pavement. Penelope sniffed excitedly and Spock trotted close, veering off once or twice to lift a leg. Near the end of the block, Poppy stopped, unable to take another step, letting Penelope finish sniffing around a tree before turning back.

Images and sensations from the day tumbled around in her mind. *Irene on her doorstep in blue satin; the horrible taste of the espresso; Fauna gently taking her biscuit and jumping onto the white sofa; on the rocks in the Wissahickon, the three dogs flopped around her; Poppy Junior being placed in Mrs. Twigg's arms; Price's bony hug; the melting glacier heart in the doctor's office; crying with Clive in the garden; the tea leaves in the cup in the playroom; the splintery floor of the tree house; Price saying, "Do you have any idea how lucky you are?"; Irene lying on the rumpled rug in a pool of pee, the blinding white of Alma's nursing uniform.*

A memory floats up, one that comes back to her, from time to time, like a riddle.

She is small, five or six, and has poured herself a glass of orange juice. When she picks up the glass, the unreal bright orange of the opaque liquid mesmerizes, she stares. *This is you, drinking,* says the voice. *No one else will ever do exactly this.* It's in her head, but it is as if someone is shouting at her. A message from herself to herself. Until now she always thought it had something to do with the orange color, but no. Now there is the blinding white of Alma's uniform. *What else do you think there is? What are you waiting for?*

A car, sleek and black, pulled up to the stop sign. Inside music pounded so loud that Poppy could see the car bounce on the downbeat. The windows were so dark she could not see the driver. Poppy could feel eyes considering her and not in a good way. Spock, growling, moved to Poppy's side and assumed his most menacing stance: ears pricked forward, tail still, body taut, ready to leap. At her feet, Penelope, prey not predator, had frozen.

Tires squealing like dark laughter, the car sped away.

Poppy walked quickly toward home. Then she was running. Penelope chuffed indignantly but kept up. Spock ran beside her, turning his head constantly, alert for threats. Poppy flew up the steps, dragging Penelope inside, Spock bounding in last.

The door closed, Poppy sank to the floor and took Penelope into her arms. Spock stood near, the warm fug of his breath on her neck, his tail wagging slowly back and forth as he waited for her to signal that all was well.

Awed by his courage, she whispered, "You are a good and brave dog. The very best."

Spock closed his mouth, twitched his ears, then gave himself a shake and sneezed on her. Poppy laughed and Penelope, sensing the crisis had passed, wriggled to be set free.

Hearing a rustling sound, Poppy looked down the hall to see Clive fiddling with a paper bag at the kitchen counter. He reached into a pocket, whisking something out, followed by more crumpling.

Then he was walking toward her holding out the bag and saying, "You forgot to open your fortune cookie."

Scrambling to her feet, Poppy said, "What about your cookie?"

"They only gave us one, so I saved it for you. We can share." He held out the bag, the edges neatly folded.

Poppy reached in and her fingers closed around the smooth satiny box she knew would be there.

"Yes," she said, her heart filling. "We can do that."

And Spock smiled his ghastly smile, not that anyone was noticing.

ACKNOWLEDGMENTS

My warmest thanks are owed to my family and friends for helping me stay the course. These include my immediate family (who have to live with me) and the extended family of siblings and cousins as well as those I miss every day—my mother and her brothers—especially my uncle, Clem Wood, a writer who loved dogs even more passionately than I do. My LibraryThing chums and my Irish music posse have been great supporters. I owe special thanks to two LibraryThingers, the late Pat Howard, an avid early reader who made sure I kept the installments coming, and my reading twin, egger-on, and dear friend, Peggy Ann McLean.

A lifetime of teachers and advisors have my gratitude. My time at Warren Wilson as a student in the MFA program was well spent, and my enduring friendship with Jim Schley began there. He has been my primary editor at Tupelo/Leapfolio for this project. Under his watchful eye I've learned to be a better and more attentive writer. I thank all the staff and Jeffrey Levine at Tupelo/Leapfolio as well. A thank you also to Martin Edmunds for reading and encouraging me. Finally a thank you to my beloved brother Owen Andrews, who read the manuscript more times than anyone else except me.

CPSIA information can be obtained
at www.ICGtesting.com
Printed in the USA
BVHW030122280520
580437BV00017B/105